CCS Investigations

Book 3 : TRAVIS

By

Susan Elle

For

Ursula Publishing UK

CCS Investigations
Book Three : Travis
Text Copyright © 2014
By Susan Elle
Ursula Publishing UK
All Rights Reserved.

Cover Photograph
Dmitriv Kiryushchenkov © /Dreamstime.com

ISBN 978-1-910753-13-2

Other Books by Susan Elle

The Sara Colson Trilogy includes

Sara's Child

Sara's Loss

Sara's Shame

All the above also available as audio books.

Catherine Colson-Sayers Investigations

CCS Investigations : Bk 1 : Missing

CCS Investigations : Bk 2 : The Chosen

CCS Investigations : Bk 3 : Travis

CCS Investigations : Bk 4 : Deleted

CCS Investigations : Bk 5 : Mind Games, due out end

Aug 2015, twice the length of previous books.

Tempest

Broken

Love, Lies & Consequences Trilogy

Book One : Love

Book Two : Lies

Book Three : Consequences

http://www.susan-elle.com/

TABLE OF CONTENTS

<u>PROLOGUE</u>

In a facility for the mentally impaired one of the 'lost' is clawing her way back from the darkest recesses of her mind.

On admission she had been combative, vocally abusive and demanding to be set free. Her strength had taken two burley security assistants to control, and even then she had been difficult to restrain.

But life in the sanatorium has a way of seeping under the skin, of setting free all those frantic thoughts and feelings...or closing them down into the deep still waters of the mind.

Cherish had bathed in those still waters, had closed her mind off to everything and everyone around her. She didn't respond when a fellow patient prodded her out of curiosity or spite, she simply sat with eyes that didn't see...at least, not in this world.

Inside her mind Cherish was free. Free to be with Travis, to enjoy his embraces and to laugh with him again.

How she loved him, her heart sang at the very thought of his handsome face and his long chestnut hair. She loved to run her hands through it, to feel its softness against her breasts as he suckled them so very gently. He had always been hers, they were meant to be together forever, she was certain of it.

But dreams and imaginings are not flesh and blood, are not as warm and comforting as the arms of a lover...of her lover...

Cherish Wade is waking up, slowly swimming to the surface of those still waters to climb out and back into the world again...

CHAPTER ONE

"Oh my..." Catherine stretches lazily next to Logan and smiles like a cat that just raided a creamery. "Is it the air here, or are you just so damn sexy that you melt my bones? I feel all...liquid somehow."

Pulling her to him, Logan slides his large hand down her smooth back and whacks her bottom playfully. "That's what good sex does for you," he laughs as she tries to wriggle out of his arms.

"I'll get you back for that," Catherine promises. Then instead of fighting to free herself she lays still and compliant against his solid body, fitting her own to his.

"That's better..." Logan sighs contentedly and hugs her to him, "...we'll have five more minutes then hit the gym. You did say you wanted me to work out with you today."

"I did, yes," she confirms, and listens for the twins in case they've begun to stir. "If we hurry we can get done and showered before the boys wake up."

Still enjoying a night feed, Adam and Andrew tend to wake around 8 for their next feed. So that gives Catherine and Logan an hour to work up a good sweat in the gym.

Pulling on jog bottoms and t-shirts, they make their way down to the new state-of-the-art gym and prepare to work hard.

"Ok, we'll do the warm-up routine as usual then I'll take you through the workout," Logan tells her, already beginning to stretch out his body in ways that have Catherine watching him, full of admiration.

Playing rugby for an amateur league side keeps Logan in trim, and his big build moves with consummate ease through a number of different stretching exercises.

Having spent so much time admiring Logan, Catherine is still finishing off after he has finished. Standing patiently, he watches her complete the routine and nods approvingly.

"You're getting right down into those calf stretches," Logan tells her. "Now we'll get down to the real business of a good sweaty workout."

For the next half hour they enjoy each other's company, pushing the limits of Catherine's abilities and finding satisfaction in their joint efforts.

"I like it when we workout together," Catherine tells Logan, lying on the floor doing the cool-down stretches he's shown her. "It's boring when I do it on my own."

"You could always workout with Emma when it isn't convenient to do so with me," Logan tells her, finishing off the last of his stretches.

"I suppose." And taking the hand that Logan is holding out to her, Catherine gets to her feet and heads to the showers with him.

Using the larger wet-room, they shower together and enjoy the shared intimacy. Catherine still finds sharing her emotions difficult, but physical intimacy with Logan has always come naturally to her.

He is hers, she is his, that's all she needs to know. And she does, right down to the very core of her being, Catherine's belief in their love is absolute.

"I thought I'd take the boys over to see Caroline and the girls today," Catherine tells Logan as they both towel off. "Do you want to come?"

"That's a good idea, yes. That's what weekends are for..." he grins happily, "...some good old fashioned family time."

Watching Logan pull on a towelling wrap, Catherine can't help smiling as she pulls on one of her own. "You're goofy happy with all this family stuff," she observes, giving him a friendly punch on the arm.

Putting an arm about her shoulders, Logan smiles down into her lovely blue eyes and nods, "Yes, I really am. In fact, I don't believe life gets much better than this."

Going back up to their bedroom, the pair dress and get ready for the day ahead. The sun is shining, life is good and the boys are beginning to stir.

By the time they finish feeding and changing the twins, Henry and Linda have already cooked a nice breakfast for them all.

Catherine and Logan put the boys in their bouncing cradles to play while they join Henry and Linda at the breakfast table.

"We were thinking of taking the boys into Sheriton for a visit with their cousins," Logan announces as they take their seats. "Is there anything you need us to pick up?"

Both Linda and Henry shake their heads but a look passes between them that sparks Catherine's interest.

"What was that?" Catherine waves her fork to point between them, "That look...like you've got some kind of a secret?"

Another look passes between Logan's father and his old housekeeper. "We were going to wait until later today to tell you to give us a chance to find out more," Henry explains. "But if you're going into Sheriton you need to know." Taking a deep breath, he tells them the news that he and Linda had heard on the radio earlier.

"There was a fire at the Mosbry Senior School. It's been deemed suspicious," Henry frowns tellingly.

"Any loss of life?" Logan asks.

"That's the thing..." Henry continues, "...the older kids were rehearsing for a play they were meant to be putting on to raise funds for the school – they've only said that lives were lost, no numbers have been given as yet."

Putting down her knife and fork, Catherine looks across at her boys and fear tears through her.

Knowing how Catherine's mind works, Logan reaches to take her hand. "Our boys are fine; nothing is going to happen to them. We'll give Caroline and Travis a call, make sure they're ok and see if there's anything we can do to help the community."

"I'll get the boys ready and in the car," Catherine says, her voice controlled, her emotions locked away.

"You could leave the boys here with us," Linda offers helpfully.

"No, the boys are coming with us," Catherine states firmly, not comfortable to have them out of her sight. "But thanks."

Moving quickly, Catherine get's the boys into their coats and tiny shoes, then pulls a cardigan on over her t-shirt and jeans.

"I'm just going to nip up to the nursery to fetch their changing bag," she tells Logan, and rushes out of the kitchen.

"I'm sorry about that," Logan nods to the wasted breakfast that Catherine had taken just a couple of mouths full of. "I'll get her to eat something at Caroline's."

"Not to worry," Henry waves his son's concern away. "Just take care of her and the boys. Did Catherine go to school at Mosbry?"

"Yes. I think that's what's upset her," Logan admits. "We'll see what's what and let you know later."

"Ok, we're ready to go," Catherine announces, and crosses to take Andrew out of his bouncy cradle.

She watches as Logan picks Adam up, holding her son tight to her chest. *You're ok my babies. You're ok. Mummy and daddy will keep you safe...I promise.*

With the boys safely fastened into their child seats in the back of the car, Logan begins the short journey to Sheriton.

This had been meant to be a happy family day, but now they are both aware that there are many families who will be suffering loss and many more a terrible anguish and fear while waiting to see if their loved ones will survive their injuries.

"What did you find out?" Logan asks, and Catherine's head shoots round to look at him.

Not bothering to deny that she'd taken the time to fire up her trusty laptop and find out all she could about the fire, Catherine gives him the latest new.

"Six died at the time of the fire...one teacher and 5 students," she recalls flatly. "Another two students have died since and 7 are in a critical condition with 2 of those not expected to survive."

It was all said matter-of-fact, not a trace of emotion anywhere.

Turning onto the motorway, Logan keeps looking straight ahead and gives Catherine time to get her thoughts together. Then he asks, "What's wrong, Catherine? Why has this affected you so deeply and on such a personal level?"

"Why?!" she asks incredulous. "You did hear what your father said, right? The fire was deemed suspicious – well now I can tell you that arson has been confirmed. There's another monster out there!"

So, now we're getting to it. Another monster; someone taking lives and causing immense suffering – you would see it like that. And maybe you're right.

"Not all monsters are yours to fight," Logan tries to reason, but knows that Catherine won't be so easily swayed. "The police and fire department have their own specialist teams of investigators. Just let them do their jobs."

Turning back to looking out of the side window, Catherine remains silent but thoughtful the rest of the way.

As they pull into the car park of The Lovett Hotel, Catherine spots Adrianne getting out of her car. "Jesus! It's a wonder she can walk now she's that big," Catherine observes, frowning with concern at her sister's efforts.

"Hmm, I'm sure Adrianne will be glad when she can carry the baby in her arms instead of her belly," Logan winces when the young woman puts both hands to the small of her back and arches backwards in a stretching motion. "She looks very uncomfortable."

"Hey, Adrianne," Catherine calls over as she climbs out of the car. "How are you doing?"

Waddling over to her big sister, Adrianne smiles ruefully, "I'm glad we're almost at the finishing post." And putting both hands on her enormously swollen abdomen, Adrianne circles her hands as if to ease the tension. "I feel huge and very clumsy. I seem to bash into everything and get covered in bruises."

Frowning, Catherine eyes her sister with concern, "But you're ok, you're not dizzy or faint?"

"No, just too wide to get through most gaps and not very good at judging the distance," Adrianne laughs.

Logan and Robert greet each other warmly and follow the women into the hotel.

"How's business..." Logan asks, "...still expanding?"

"We certainly are," Robert grins. "Good job I'm a bit of a workaholic really, there's so much to do and not all of it to do with work. I just finished getting the nursery how Adrianne wants it and we picked up the last of the essentials for the baby last weekend. Now we're just waiting for the little blighter to arrive."

Chuckling deeply, Logan gives Robert a pat on the back as they carry the twins in their car seats.

When they step off the lift into the penthouse, the sisters all embrace excitedly.

"Look at you…" Caroline holds Adrianne's hands and admires her baby bump, "…it won't be long now, the baby looks lower than it did the last time we met up!"

"The heads engaged," Adrianne declares proudly.

"You look beautiful," Travis declares, hugging his sister-in-law tentatively. "Why don't you take a seat and I'll send for some tea – or would you prefer something else?" he asks, looking around his guests.

"A nice cup of her ladyship's tea would go down a treat," Catherine replies, giving a nod towards Caroline.

"Actually, I'd love a glass of cold milk," Adrianne pipes up. "I find it settles me," she smiles up at Travis.

The chatter is happy and Caroline hands Adrianne one of the girls, while Catherine looks round expectantly.

Travis brings the other little girl and lays her in her aunt's open arms. "Hey, Leanne," Catherine touches her finger to the baby's soft cheek. "You get more beautiful every time I see you. And just look at that smile, you're a little angel."

"I think Sara likes my hair," Adrianne grimaces, pulling her long black hair from the baby's grip and shoving it out of reach over her shoulder.

"Tell me about it," Caroline grins. "When I was feeding her earlier, she all but scalped me."

"I can attest to the fact that Sara does seem to have a fascination for hair," Travis smiles ruefully, touching a hand to his long chestnut hair. "Leanne seems to like jewellery; her little hands always seem to find a necklace, watch or ring to play with."

"What about the boys, are either of them hair pullers," Caroline asks.

"I think that's a girl thing," Robert observes with a grin.

"Not at all..." Catherine lifts her chin proudly, "...I always found a fist square in the face to be much more effective."

After a moment's stunned silence, everyone breaks into peals of laughter that leave Catherine blushing.

"Only you, my darling," Logan grins over at her.

"Well they didn't come back for seconds," she defends with a frown. Looking down at the little girl in her arms, Catherine whispers, "Don't you worry, Aunty Catherine will teach you how to deal with bullies, and you won't be pulling hair either!"

CHAPTER TWO

Following Logan into the kitchen area of the penthouse, Caroline takes the opportunity to voice the concerns she has for her sister.

"What's wrong with Catherine?" she asks bluntly. "For all her happy chatter I can see there's something eating at her. What is it?"

They may have come together only recently, but the two women are identical twins and seem to be able to sense each other's feelings and emotions pretty accurately.

"She's worrying about the arson attack on the school; I'm not entirely sure why, but Catherine has taken it very hard," Logan admits with a grimace.

Letting out a long breath, Caroline nods and her expression turns grim. "I heard about that on the morning news. It sounded bloody awful. I can't imagine what kind of monster would do that."

"That's what Catherine called him...a monster. And I think that's the real problem," he tells Caroline while pouring boiled water into one of the two sterile bottles that he's set out on the work surface. "The arsonist may not have tortured people the way Edwards did, but to her it's all the same. Now she'll have to find him and make sure he pays for the lives he's taken and the suffering he's caused."

"Well, I can't blame her for that," Caroline sighs, relieved to understand what is troubling her sister. "Will you try to dissuade her – or will you accept the inevitable and help her instead?"

Chuckling as he screws the teat caps onto the two bottles, Logan shakes his head, "No point in trying to dissuade Catherine once she's made up her mind about something. So I suppose I'll be helping her as best I can."

Getting a couple of jugs out of a cupboard, Caroline puts one bottle into each of them and turns on the cold tap. "Just leave them here to cool for a while," she advises Logan, and putting her arm through his walks back to the lounge.

Although Catherine is enjoying the family catch up time, her mind keeps going to the school and the tragedy that happened there.

How will the parents cope? I can't image the pain of losing a child...if it had been Adam or Andrew... Oh God, please don't let anything happen to my boys.

Trying to focus on the chatter going on all around her, Catherine pulls her mind back from the precipice of despair but it isn't long before her mind turns back to the school and the disaster that had taken place there.

"I need to go out for a while," she declares, standing suddenly and handing her niece over to her father. "I shouldn't be gone long, just need to get some air."

Crossing to the lift, Catherine presses the call button and mentally wills it to hurry up.

Feeling her arm taken by a large hand, Catherine looks up into her husband's concerned brown eyes.

"I'm coming with you," he declares quietly. "The boys are fine here. Caroline knows what's going on and she's ok with you taking some time out to look into things. Though she draws the line at breastfeeding our babies," he chuckles as they step into the lift together.

"I bet," Catherine actually smiles. "I just want to see the school for myself, get a sense of what happened...you know?"

"I do." And Logan pulls her into his side, accepting that his wife has a lot of troubled emotions going around in her head that she doesn't often express openly.

She had seen the photos on the news website, had thought herself prepared for what she was about to do, but Catherine is shocked beyond belief to witness the extent of the disaster with her own eyes.

"How did it get this bad?" she asks no one in particular. "No wonder so many people died."

Despite the efforts of multiple fire engines, the school has been left a burned out shell. Not one classroom has been left intact, not one window left unbroken.

They are not the only people looking shocked and appalled by the act of a madman. Many people have come to see for themselves something so tragic that their minds could not take it in without the evidence of their own eyes.

Turning to watch a little boy lay a bouquet of flowers next to rows of others, Catherine has to choke back her tears.

There are photos taped to the school railings, the flowers laid below them in tribute.

"I'm going to catch this bastard if it's the last thing I do!" Catherine's oath is a quiet one but Logan hears her and agrees.

"We need to find out what help we can offer the families," he tells her just as quietly. "Then we'll go home and begin our own investigation."

"Just wait, I want to take some photos," Catherine tells him and earns a questioning frown from Logan. "Arsonists often like to view their handy work – he was probably here last night, enjoying the bloody show!"

"Just try to be discreet," Logan warns, not wanting to upset the people nearby.

Moving away, Catherine lifts her mobile and zooms in on the crowd to take the photos. Then, looking around them, she turns it to take more of anyone standing in the near vicinity. And finally, she takes a photo of the railings with the photos taped to them and the flowers on the ground beneath.

"Ok, I've got enough to be working on for now," Catherine tells Logan as they walk back to the hotel.

I'll get into the fire department's report and the police files to find out what the media hasn't already been told. Then I'll check for any recent arson attacks, not just schools but anywhere lives have been lost within a 50 mile radius.

I doubt this was an act of vandalism by kids – more likely someone with a grudge or on a spree. Christ I hope not!

Catherine's heart feels heavy with sadness and grief. She may not have known any of the dead personally, but she has enough compassion to empathise with the terrible grief she knows their relatives will be suffering.

To have watched your children grow into young adults, to have nurtured them and their dreams of a bright future, and then to lose all of that because of one crazy incomprehensible act of insanity...how can anyone survive that...how can they find the will to take their next breath...

Stepping back into the hotel, Catherine and Logan go up to the penthouse with grateful hearts that their family is safe.

"Can I use your bedroom to feed the boys," Catherine asks before anyone can ask her questions that she would rather not answer just now.

"Of course," Caroline tells her, getting to her feet to make sure her sister has everything she needs. "I'll bring you both in a cup of tea and a biscuit — just settle yourselves comfortably and I'll be right back."

Taking Adam first, Catherine puts him to her bared breast and feels so much love flow right through her body and into his that it scares her.

"We shouldn't have done this, how can we keep them safe when there are so many monsters in the world," Catherine states, speaking her fears out loud.

"Don't do that," Logan chides her softly. "Don't wish our boys away. We'll love them and care for them and give them the best lives that we can. The rest is up to God."

Her blue eyes flash with anger as she looks over at Logan, who has settled himself and Andrew on a chair nearby.

"Then God had better get his act together! If anyone so much as thinks about hurting our boys I'll make them wish they'd never been born — and then God can have what's left of them," Catherine adds menacingly.

Stroking Andrew's back as he lies over his broad shoulder, Logan considers Catherine and her fierce protective instincts.

"And you said you wouldn't make a very good mother," he shakes his head and chuckles softly. "You're a fine woman and a wonderful mother — stop borrowing trouble and enjoy our sons. They'll grow up all too soon and then we'll lose them to university and the wider world."

Frowning deeply, Catherine looks down at Adam, suckling at her breast, and strokes a gentle hand over his head. *You may go off to university, but your home will always be here. Even if you do get sidetracked for a while like your dad did.*

Much later that evening, after giving her boys their last feed before bed time, Catherine sits at her desk and begins the delicate task of hacking into the police and fire departments records.

Logan is working at Emma's desk, his laptop open and a glass of white wine within easy reach.

Reading the fire department report first, Catherine is shocked to see the photographs taken of the scene once the fire had been put out.

Clicking through them she lets out a gasp and sits back in her seat, staring at the screen with incredulous eyes.

"You ok? What is it?" Logan asks, looking over at Catherine then getting to his feet when she only silently shakes her head.

Moving behind Catherine, he looks over her shoulder at what has caught her attention and obviously upset her.

"Good Lord! That wasn't mentioned in the press or on the news, I'm sure of it," Logan states emphatically.

"No, and I can see why," Catherine murmurs softly. "They wouldn't want to encourage a copy-cat."

"Heaven forbid!"

"This wasn't just about setting a fire and watching it burn," Catherine observes, not able to tear her eyes away from the picture that tells the horrible truth. "They knew there were people inside and made sure they couldn't get out easily. From what I can make out, the ones that did escape the blaze did so by smashing windows and climbing out. But not before panicking, as the arsonist intended."

"They panicked..." she continues after taking a few deep breaths. "The smoke would have been thick, filling the corridors leading to confusion and disorientation."

Flicking back to the report, Catherine finds what she is looking for and shows Logan.

"Good grief!"

Some of the victims had gone in entirely the wrong direction, ending up suffocating on the smoke and dying in the corridors. But four had made it to the main doors, their blood soaked fingers clawing until their nails had been torn away.

"One of those four survived..." Catherine points out, "...the one at the bottom of the pile and closest to the bottom of the doors."

"You were right," Logan straightens up to cross the room and gets his wine. Taking a large gulp of it, he closes his eyes but can't erase the pictures from his mind's eye.

"About what?" she asks eventually.

"He is a monster," Logan bites out, then tips up his wine glass to drain it.

Under the cloak of invisibility that the dark night affords those who know how to use it, the monster is once again roaming the streets of Sheriton, set on causing even more deaths and an even deeper fear run in the hearts of the small town's residents.

"You sent me away...had me locked up and didn't give a damn what became of me. Well...now we'll see," the shadow laughs softly, drawing an iron bar through a pair of outer door handles, "...yes indeedy, we'll just see..."

A new blockbuster film had drawn in the crowds all week, but this is Saturday night and the cinema is full very near to capacity.

CHAPTER THREE

The sound of many loud sirens awoke the residents of The Lovett Hotel that night, including Travis and Caroline.

"What on earth can be going on?" Caroline asks her husband while pulling on a housecoat.

Standing at one of the large windows, Travis looks towards the town and his stomach churns.

"There's a fire blazing in the town," he tells her sadly. "It looks to be a big one; I should go and offer assistance."

"Yes," Caroline agrees quickly. "We have spare rooms if anyone has need of them," she reminds him. "I'll get things prepared just in case."

Crossing back to the bedroom, Travis dresses quickly then takes his leave.

Thankfully the main town is only a short walk away, and the blazing cinema is on the outskirts nearest to The Lovett.

Flames are leaping high in the sky, smoke spiralling up into the night...thick and black and deadly.

"Is there anything I can do to help?" Travis asks a fire officer who looks to be in some authority.

"No, sir, but thanks for offering," the officer dismisses firmly. "If you could just stand right back, we'll get this under control."

The man made to walk away, but Travis quickly puts a hand to his arm to detain him briefly. "I own a large hotel, if any of your men or members of the public need a place for respite, they will be very welcome. The Lovett Hotel is on the left just a hundred yards or so up that street," he explains, pointing the way.

"That's good of you, I think we may have need of somewhere to take a brief rest – this fire is going to take a long time to get under control," the fire chief thanks him. "I'll get one of my men to organise it."

He'd been right; it had taken most of the night to put the blaze out. It hadn't been just the cinema that had gone up – the flames had spread to a clothes shop adjoining the property and that too had been gutted.

But no one was thinking about financial loss in the grim light of day. Over 150 people are thought to have lost their lives; the number yet to be confirmed. There had been a few lucky survivors taken by ambulance to the city hospital, but not all of those had survived the night.

A sound that Travis will never forget is the wailing of the many relatives that had gathered as close to the cinema as they'd been allowed – each one desperate to know if their son or daughter, husband or wife, friend or neighbour, had perished in the cinema.

He'd tried to comfort one woman who had fallen to the ground, her grief so profound that her legs could no longer hold her up. And so he had sat himself on the ground beside her, holding the woman's shoulders and rocking her gently, absorbing the racking sobs that had torn from her unendingly.

At one point he had suggested that she might be better waiting for news at his hotel, but the woman had been adamant about staying.

Most of the devastated relatives had said the same, but some were convinced by other family members to take up the offer and made their way to The Lovett.

Once there, Caroline, and the staff members she had enlisted, took care of them, offering food and drink and a place to sit and rest.

Those who wanted to make use of a bed were shown to the hotel's vacant rooms, but most just wanted a quiet place to sit.

It was a tragedy such as the town had never known before. And coming on the heels of the school disaster, made it all the more painful to bear.

Local people pulled out all the stops, bringing the firemen and the police officers at the scene hot and cold drinks to sustain them. Some of them made their way to The Lovett, offering to help the staff look after the people gathered there and still more tried to minister to the grieving crowd of relatives that wouldn't leave.

One such person is Cherish Wade — tall, slim and dressed plainly, she blends in at the hotel unnoticed.

Now a shocked silence is settling over the scene. Caroline is worn out, pure adrenaline the only thing keeping her going.

Luckily her babies have slept through the whole event, one of the female night staff having stayed with them to free Caroline up to take charge downstairs.

Watching a young woman hold a cup of tea to the lips of an older woman whose hands still shook too badly to hold it herself, Caroline has to wonder at the generous spirit that has prompted so many people to come out of their homes to tend to strangers in need.

All this pain and suffering caused by one person's twisted mind. It has to be the same person – it would be the biggest coincidence ever known for two different people to set these fires in as many days.

I can't even begin to think why they would have done it – nothing can justify their actions. I just hope this is an end to it!

But Caroline has a very bad feeling that the arsonist might strike again. *Unless Catherine or the police catch him first - I pray that they will.*

"You've been here most of the night, have you had anything to eat and drink yourself?" Caroline asks one of the women helping tend people.

"I'm fine," the young woman smiles pleasantly, her tired eyes belying her words as she tries in vain to stifle a yawn.

"No, you really aren't," Caroline frowns with concern. "Please, take a rest and get something inside you – you won't be able to help if you collapse," she adds with a grim smile of encouragement.

"Ok, I will if you will," the woman smiles.

"Deal," Caroline laughs companionably. "Let's go through to the restaurant and find a quiet corner."

Together they help themselves to tea and biscuits, though there is much more on offer. The hotel staff has put together a selection of sandwiches, savouries and small cakes to tempt those in need to eat and drink.

"Are you the hotel manager?" the woman asks as they take their seats out of the way of the main crowd of people.

"No, I'm married to the owner," Caroline supplies happily, then holds out a hand to the stranger.

"My name is Caroline Lovett; it's my husband Travis Lovett who owns the hotel," she smiles.

Taking the hand, the woman returns Caroline's smile easily and introduces herself. "Hi, I'm Cherish Wade, nice to meet you."

And they laugh tiredly, aware that they've been working alongside each other all night so they've hardly just met.

"I must admit, now that I'm sat down with this lovely cup of tea, I'm more tired than I realised," Cherish confesses, and goes on to give a huge yawn.

"Can I get someone to take you home?" Caroline asks, concerned for the young woman.

"No, don't trouble, though I think I will get off if you don't need me anymore," Cherish sighs heavily.

"I'll be going up myself in a minute," Caroline admits. "I just want to hand over to our manager and then I'm off to see my girls."

Standing together, they walk through the crowds of people, some of them with their heads in their hands, others curled up on the comfy settees near the bar, and yet more just sitting and staring, their eyes vague and shoulders slumped forlornly.

"It's such a terrible thing to happen," Cherish sighs sadly, looking around the devastated people.

"Yes, I can't imagine how it happened and I just can't allow myself to think about how all those people died. Though I'm sure it will get into my head once I stand still long enough," Caroline shivers, chilled by the thought.

Travis is also tired; his mind heart and soul feel heavy with the grief and tragedy surrounding him.

Once the fire had finally been put out, the fire department had erected screens to keep prying eyes out of the scene, and to spare the loved ones of those who had perished the anguish of watching the recovery of their bodies...or what was left of them.

The stink of burned flesh still hangs heavy in the air and Travis finally admits to himself that there isn't anything more that he can do.

"I'm going back to the hotel to get a shower and fall into bed," Travis tells one of the police officers on scene. "You're men are still welcome to use the hotel's facilities as and when they need to."

"That's very kind of you, Mr Lovett," the officer thanks him. "I'll make sure to pass that on. And thank you, for all the help you've been. I'm sure it's meant a lot to the people here that so many locals have come out, the way they have, to tend to their needs. It highlights the more compassionate side of the human spirit, don't you think?"

"I do," Travis agrees. "And if this proves to be arson, like the school, we're going to need to cling to that thought. Such a vile act would settle heavily on the town."

The officer looks at Travis assessingly, then confides, "Between you and me, arson has already been confirmed. All exits from the building had been barred, just like the school – those poor bastards didn't stand a chance!"

Heaving out a heavy sigh, Travis stands with his eyes closed and nods. "I thought as much, but I suppose it's only human to have hoped I was wrong."

Raising a hand to clap Travis on the back, the officer thanks him again then goes back to the dreadful scene.

The walk back to the hotel seems longer than it's ever been. Travis' feet move like lead, his stride slow and weary.

Looking up to the sky, he can see that the sun is just trying to break through, the heavy clouds of smoke that had hung over the town now cleared, only their stench left behind.

It seems indecent to have sunshine on such a bleak day. I hope Caroline's night hasn't been as draining, though she sounded tired enough the last time I phoned.

I need to see my girls, to hold them close and Caroline too. A tragedy like this makes all of us appreciate what we are lucky enough to still have - so many have lost so much.

"Mr Travis..." his manageress greets him as he enters the hotel, "...you look done in. Everything is under control here if you want to go straight up."

Nodding, and giving her the merest of smiles, Travis looks around the foyer and sees the exhausted faces of police and fire officers mingled with those of the grieving relatives who were still waiting for news from the fire scene.

But he is too tired to linger, too emotionally drained to offer more to these people, though his heart bleeds for them.

"Is Caroline with the girls..?"

"I believe so," the manageress nods. "She gave me an update of what has been going on and instructions for what else needs to be done then disappeared. I wouldn't be surprised if Miss Caroline isn't flat out on the bed – she looked every bit as tired as you do now."

"Ok, thanks – and make sure that our staff knows how much we appreciate their extraordinary efforts," Travis tells her, then makes his way to the penthouse lift.

Just standing upright in the lift seems to take a great deal of effort, and Travis rubs his large hands roughly over his face in a bid to wake himself up long enough to greet his family.

Jeanine, from the night staff, is sitting on one of the large settees giving Leanne her morning bottle, and Sara is sat in her bouncing chair at her feet, having already been fed.

"Thank you for helping out, Jeanine," Travis smiles as he crosses the room. Bending to pick up Sara, he carries her to the other settee and settles himself with her cradled into his neck.

"Is Caroline asleep?" he asks, breathing in the wonderful familiarity of his daughter's scent and wallowing in the normality of the moment.

When Jeanine doesn't immediately answer, Travis looks over at her with a quizzically raised brow.

"I thought Miss Caroline was still working downstairs," Jeanine tells him, using the staff's usual term when referring to the boss' wife.

"So, when did you last see her?" Travis asks, concerned that his wife is wearing herself out somewhere.

"Miss Caroline came up a couple of hours ago – she asked me to let her know if the girls stirred so that she could come and see them for a little bit," Jeanine smiles, recalling how loving Miss Caroline had been with the twins. "I rang down to reception about half an hour ago, but they said she was really busy and they'd let her know."

"Alright, I'll give her another couple of minutes then I'll go down and get her," Travis smiles ruefully. "Caroline will carry on until she drops otherwise."

A couple of minutes soon turn into ten; Travis is enjoying the time with his daughter so much.

"Come on, Sara, let's go and look for mummy," he croons, crossing the room with the baby still settled over his shoulder. Once in the lift he presses for the ground floor and leans back against the mirrored wall.

"Mr Travis..." his manageress says with some surprise as he walks towards her, "...I thought you were going up for some rest?"

"I was," he agrees, then gives her a lopsided smile. "And I will, once I find my wife. Caroline just doesn't know when to quit!"

Frowning up at him, the stout woman shakes her head and says, "But Miss Caroline isn't down here – are you sure she isn't already in bed?"

"Jeanine said she hasn't been back to the penthouse in a couple of hours or so – she must be down here," he frowns, tiredness making him unusually annoyed. "I'll take a look in the restaurant; you call around the other areas and let me know if you find her." Then he strides away, Sara now fast asleep on her daddy's shoulder.

But after a short time it becomes clear that Caroline isn't in the hotel or on its grounds – a couple of porters having searched the gardens just in case she had gone outside to get some air.

"What the hell is going on?!" Travis demands, his tired mind barely able to comprehend the situation. "Surely someone knows where she's gone?!"

Then a new young porter puts his hand up like he's in school and pipes up, "Miss Caroline said she was giving someone a lift home – one of the volunteers, I think."

"And how long ago was that?" Travis asks, feeling somewhat relieved.

"Not sure, sir," the porter steps forward hesitantly. "About an hour ago, I think."

"Ok then..." he sighs heavily, "...I'll be up in the penthouse – make sure my wife comes up directly she gets back."

<u>CHAPTER FOUR</u>

With Emma away at her parent's for the weekend, Catherine and Logan are working alone to find all the info they can on recent arson cases in the local area.

"I wonder if Emma's heard about the school going up in flames," Catherine murmurs, her fingers still dancing over the keyboard of her souped-up laptop.

"It made the national news, so I image she has," Logan replies, his brow furrowed as he reads of another arson attack in a neighbouring village. But he doesn't think it's linked to the person who torched the school as it happened over two years ago.

"Holy shit!" Catherine suddenly gasps, Logan crossing to her side to see what she's found. "What the hell is going on – I can't believe what I'm reading!"

What she is reading is the fire department's preliminary report on the fire at the school – only now there has been an addendum added; a fire at a local cinema is thought to be the work of the same person with a loss of life numbering 156 so far.

"This happened last night," Logan reads, his stomach feeling like a lead weight has settled in it. "The fire alarm was raised at 11:20 p.m. - the exits were deliberately sealed, the same way they had been at the school."

"Someone is intentionally killing people – as many people as they can, by the looks of this." Catherine stares at the report, her thoughts struggling to be coherent as the magnitude of what they are up against begins to sink in.

Please God, no more. Don't let there be any more. All of those poor people terrified and burned alive. How could anyone in their right minds do such a thing, and then deliberately do it again? Surely this is not just arson, there has to be a reason behind it.

"Catherine, are you alright?" Logan is staring at her, looking very concerned.

"Yes, of course, why...?" she replies dazedly.

"Because I asked you a question and you didn't seem to hear me," Logan tells her, still looking worried.

"I was just thinking...we need to find a connection...we need to work out what this maniac wants...what point he's trying to make," Catherine muses out loud, her fingers working on her keyboard again.

The fire report disappears from her screen, replaced by the photos she had taken of the burned out school and the people in attendance at the same time as they had been there.

Then she hits a key that sends the images to the printer and crosses to take each picture, as it emerges, and pin it up on one of the whiteboards.

"We need more," Catherine declares, barely noticing Logan's presence, her brilliant mind working faster than her hands can keep up.

Back at her laptop, she hacks into the television station that broadcast the video report on the school fire and downloads a copy of it. Then she looks for any video pertaining to the cinema blaze and doesn't take the time to be shocked by it.

Logan can see that Catherine has forgotten him, focused on a train of thought that he doesn't want to distract her from. And so he goes back to Emma's desk and continues with his search for previous arson attacks that might be linked to the ones in Sheriton.

But he keeps an eye on Catherine, watching her work frantically, almost manically, driven by the need to put a stop to the terrible carnage.

And then it comes, a phone call that will shock everyone to the core, even more than the terrible deaths of so many people.

"Hi, Travis…" Logan greets his brother-in-law, "…everything ok?"

But even before Travis can answer, Logan watches Catherine come to an abrupt stop, turning to him with large eyes and her face gone pale.

"Caroline!" she gasps, and falls to her knees.

"Yes, yes, we'll be right there," Logan tells a distraught Travis. "Did you call the police? Ok, yes, I'll tell her," Logan listens to Travis for another few seconds then puts the phone down and crosses to his wife.

"She's in terrible danger – I can feel it," Catherine mumbles, looking at Logan like she's looking through him. "Why didn't I feel it before…? Oh God, please don't let anything happen to my sister!"

"I'm not surprised you didn't feel it, you've been concentrating so hard on what you've been working on you probably blocked it out," Logan tells her gently.

"Blocked out my own sister?!" Catherine gets to her feet abruptly, heart racing, her mind clawing at her jangled thoughts to stop them going off in all directions. "We need to go. We need to get to Sheriton as fast as we can. Did he call Adrianne too?" she asks as they make their way downstairs.

"He said not. I think he was worried it might be too much for her in her present state," Logan explains.

"Present state...?" Catherine frowns up at him as they reach the hallway.

"The fact that she is due to give birth any time soon," Logan clarifies, his expression telling Catherine that she isn't behaving normally.

Looking stricken, Catherine shakes her head and asks, "What the hell is wrong with me...why is my brain so out of sync?"

"Don't worry about it. Just try to relax and let me do the thinking for now," Logan tells her, and is surprised when Catherine doesn't protest.

Something is very wrong for Catherine to let that go unchallenged. She really doesn't seem to be able to think straight, and not just in an absent minded way.

I think this may have to do with some disruption to their specific bond and to Catherine's ability to 'see' things.

Jesus...what the hell do I know about such things. Until Catherine, I didn't even believe in psychic abilities...now...I just don't have a clue how to help her!

Going down to the kitchen, Logan and Catherine go in search of Henry and Linda to let them know about the cinema disaster.

Henry is out in the back garden, feeding the chickens and searching for fresh laid eggs.

"Morning you two..." he smiles happily, "...I'm just getting some nice fresh eggs to start breakfast."

But when he straightens and looks at them properly, Henry can see that something is very much amiss. "What's wrong, did you find out something bad about the school fire?"

"You've not had the radio on this morning?" Logan asks, knowing that it is his father's usual habit.

"No, no, Linda and I didn't want to hear any more reports about the school," he admits sadly. "I know the media have a job to do but it seemed to be repeated every five minutes on the radio, so we decided not to have it on today."

"There's been another fire, even worse than the school fire," Logan explains, still holding Catherine's hand and feeling how cold she is.

"What?!"

"It was the cinema; it happened late last night. There was almost a full house for the latest blockbuster and with it being Saturday night," Logan rubs his free hand over his eyes, not wanting to tell this latest bad news but knowing that he must. "Someone set the fire and sealed the doors, just like they did at the school," Logan tells his father, watching as he loses all colour, "156 people have died and Caroline has gone missing," he adds, turning to look at Catherine who hasn't said a word.

"156 people...?" Henry repeats dazedly. "And what's this about Caroline, what do you mean...missing?"

Just then, Linda comes into the garden having been for an early morning walk by the lake. Her contented smile slips and a frown draws a shadow over her eyes, "Missing...did you say Caroline is missing?"

"We need to get to Sheriton; would you mind looking after the boys today – there's still plenty of Catherine's milk in the freezer – the tubs are all dated," Logan tells Linda hurriedly. "I'll leave dad to explain the rest, thought you can't tell anyone else about the sealed doors – that information hasn't been released to the public," he adds before turning with Catherine and making their way out to his car.

"Sealed doors...?" Linda looks at Henry quizzically then her face pales markedly. "The school doors had been sealed...?" she asks breathily, then her legs go from under her and Linda sits heavily down on the pathway.

Crossing to her side quickly, Henry crouches down to take her hand, "Come along, we'll have a strong cup of tea and I'll tell you all about it."

The telling of the whole tale is punctuated with regular gasps of shock and a steady flow of sorrowful tears from Linda.

"I can hardly believe my ears," Linda sniffs, blowing her nose on the tissues that Henry has given her. "All those poor people – and Caroline missing too."

"I don't honestly know what one thing has to do with the other, but the way Logan said it, it sounds like Caroline's disappearance is linked to the fire somehow," Henry muses, trying to think back over what Logan had said.

"This isn't an end to it..." Linda tells him, shaking her head, "...someone is on a mission, exacting revenge for some supposed wrong that was done against them or a loved one."

"Catherine looked to be in shock..." Henry observes over his teacup, "...I don't imagine she will be much help in finding out who is doing this."

But Linda shakes her head, her eyes narrowed in thought, "Don't you believe it. Catherine and Caroline have a very deep bond, one that isn't understood by those not privy to the ways of identical twins," she adds mysteriously. "If Caroline is truly missing, her best chance of being found is through Catherine. Taking Caroline could be the arsonist's biggest mistake," Linda tells Henry with a firm nod of her head.

Not at all sure that Linda isn't just grasping at straws, Henry refills their cups with more tea as he thinks about what she's said. "So, you actually believe that the twins can use this 'bond' to communicate with each other in some way – like tuning in to each other's thoughts?"

Heaving a large sigh, Linda shakes her head, "I don't have the faintest idea how it works, but I do know that it has been well documented, this connection that twins have," she explains. "Even non-identical twins have been known to 'feel' or 'sense' when their twin has been seriously injured, is in danger or has died."

Lifting a brow, Henry nods in agreement, "Sounds like you could be right then – taking Caroline could be this murderer's biggest mistake!"

CHAPTER FIVE

Pulling into the hotel's car park, Logan struggles to find a vacant parking spot and has to pull round the side of the hotel.

A lot of people are still milling around the building with media vans and police cars taking up a lot of the parking spaces.

"Don't speak to anyone," Logan advises when they alight the car and he comes around to take Catherine's arm. "We'll go straight up to the penthouse and see Travis."

The lobby of the hotel still has a lot of people from the cinema disaster being tended to by the hotel's staff, but they wind their way through unhindered. But before they reach the penthouse lift, a young porter shouts over in obvious relief.

"Miss Caroline! Miss Caroline!" A porter rushes to Catherine's side, his grin stretching from ear to ear. "Mr Travis has been worried sick...I'll get the desk to ring up and tell him you're back, shall I?"

If possible, Catherine pales still further and Logan fears she may faint.

"This is Catherine..." Logan explains kindly, "...Miss Caroline's identical twin."

The young man looks shocked and then deflates as realisation dawns, "Sorry, Miss, I didn't know..."

Moving on, Logan presses for the lift and watches Catherine with eyes darkened by concern. She still hasn't spoken a word, not all the way from Lakelands and not even when the boy mistook her for Caroline.

Stepping off the lift and into the penthouse, Logan guides her to a settee and gently pushes her down onto it.

"Catherine, are you alright?" Travis asks, coming out of the girls' bedroom and crossing to sit beside her. "I'm so sorry to worry you, but it isn't like Caroline not to be in touch after this amount of time," he tells her. "And no one seems to know who the volunteer was that she took home, so we can't even check with them that she's still there – but it's a possibility," he adds hopefully.

But Catherine is shaking her head, then finally finds her voice. "The first thing I felt from Caroline was fear and a sense of great danger," Catherine tells him, her lips beginning to tremble but no tears are allowed to fall. "And I've been trying hard to reconnect with her, but I'm not getting anything...not a damn thing!"

So that's why you've been so quiet. Logan moves to sit at his wife's other side and takes her hand. *I've been going out of my mind with worry that you were going into yourself like before.*

"Perhaps if you go into Caroline and Travis' bedroom – just be around her things...?" Logan suggests quietly.

Nodding in agreement, Travis says, "I think that might be a good idea. We could leave you in peace so as not to disturb your thoughts, and feel free to look through anything you think might help you."

"Ok..." Catherine nods, "...I'll give it a try."

Walking into the bedroom, Catherine moves to the wall of fitted wardrobes and fingers her sister's dresses, and other garments, in a bid to make some sort of connection...but she get's nothing.

Wandering the room, she picks up framed photographs of Caroline's babies and tries to tap into the love that her sister would have felt every time she looked into them...but again she get's nothing.

For a long time Catherine lays on the side of the bed where she knows her sister sleeps and tries to calm her mind, hoping to make some contact. After an hour of desperate concentration, Catherine gets up and moves to sit at her sister's dressing table and touches the bottles and other accessories she finds there.

Looking into the mirror, Catherine reaches out to touch her reflection, a dreadful, soul deep sadness filling her heart.

Where are you, Caroline...why can't I feel you? Is our connection so new and tenuous that it can be broken so easily? Or is there something I'm missing, something I should be doing to make our connection work? I can't think...I can't get past the pain...

But maybe you can feel me; I have to hope that you can. Don't lose hope, Caroline, I'm going to find you and bring you home...I promise. I promise you with everything that I am, I will bring you home!

Going back into the main lounge area, Catherine sees two pair of eyes watching her intently as she crosses the room.

"I'm sorry, Travis, it didn't work," she tells him. And looking over into her husband's eyes, Catherine's sorrow is clearly evident.

"What about Farraday?" Logan suggests, the idea hitting him out of the blue. "You seem to have some sort of psychic rapport with the man – maybe he could help you to find Caroline?"

Her mouth falling open, Catherine's blue eyes round in astonishment, "I didn't think of him! Oh Logan, do you think he'd be willing to help us?"

Travis looks at his sister-in-law in confusion, "Who is Farraday, and how could he possibly help us?"

"He's a psychic – a vision walker, actually," she clarifies, then sees that she has confused Travis even more. "Neil gets visions of incidents that have happened or are about to happen. Unfortunately, he not only gets to see what happened but actually walks through the scene and experiences the tragedy as if he's really there."

"Good lord!" Travis exclaims, blowing out a long breath. "And you think this man may be able to do this to find Caroline?"

Looking hesitant, Catherine sits beside Travis and takes his hand, "I don't know. But I do know that the last time I worked with Neil, he was able to guide my own skills and made them stronger, magnifying them somehow."

"Skills? You have psychic abilities?" Travis asks, not as shocked as Catherine might have expected.

"I don't know about that..." Catherine frowns, not liking the sound of that suggestion, "...but I do 'feel' things sometimes. Like knowing who's on the phone before I pick it up," she smiles, liking that explanation better.

"Can we get in touch with this Farraday chap?" Travis asks hopefully.

"We can give it a try." And Catherine takes out her mobile and brings up the psychic's number.

Not five minutes later, Logan is pulling the Range Rover out of the hotel's car park and driving Catherine to Neil Farraday's house.

He's heard about the arson attacks and is more than willing to help in any way he can. When they pull up outside of his house, Neil comes quickly to the front door and lets them in.

"Come in, come in," he bids them eagerly, and shows them through to his sitting room. "I don't know what I can do; I haven't received anything to do with these attacks..." he tells them, referring to his psychic abilities to receive visions, "...but I might be able to tap into them through you."

Nodding her agreement, Catherine says, "That's what we were hoping for."

"Ok, take a seat and tell me everything you can," Neil waves a hand to indicate the settee while he takes a seat in an armchair nearby.

It takes a while to work her way through the details of the school fire and then the cinema fire, but Catherine feels it's important to tell Neil everything.

"I got one flash of...of...emotion, I suppose," Catherine frowns, struggling to find the right words to describe her earlier connection to Caroline. "I could discern fear and terrible danger, but I haven't felt anything since. Why?" she asks earnestly, feeling that she is failing Caroline miserably.

Pursing his lips, Neil takes the time to think things through then tells Catherine and Logan his conclusions. "There are a few possibilities that I can think of," he begins thoughtfully. "Firstly, if Caroline is being held against her will, it is possible that she is being sedated, making your connection with her tenuous at best."

"Christ, I didn't think of that!" Catherine expounds, shocked to her core.

"There's also the possibility that your heightened stress levels are preventing you from reaching out to your sister, inadvertently blocking the connection," Neil suggests.

"Yes, I have thought of that and tried to clear my mind while I was lying on Caroline's bed – but I still didn't get anything," Catherine sighs heavily.

Shifting uncomfortably in his seat, Neil is reluctant to voice his final thought, but sees no help for it. "Or your sister might have been killed."

That suggestion has Catherine paling visibly, and Logan squeezes her hand reassuringly.

"No..." she states with conviction, "...I would know that. I would have felt the loss," she adds, her eyes defiant as they bore into Neil's.

Putting up a hand, palm out in defence, Neil tries to explain further. "I'm just voicing all of the possibilities — though I tend to agree, the last is unlikely."

"It's impossible is what it is," Catherine states unyieldingly.

"Quite so," Neil acquiesces hurriedly. "Now, perhaps we should try to reach out to Caroline together — use our combined strengths to magnify the signal, as it were," he suggests hopefully.

"Yes, that's what I was thinking," Catherine agrees eagerly. "Maybe you can help me to get past this infernal block."

Changing places with Logan, Neil moves to sit beside Catherine and joins their hands. "Ok, close your eyes and let me in — relax your body and try not to think of anything but a blank page. Yes...that's it, that's it," he repeats as their minds join.

"Ok, now I want you to visualise a brick wall behind which Caroline stands," he instructs, his tone of voice soft and deep, almost monotone. "Yes, that's it – now I want you to imagine that you're holding a sledge hammer and begin breaking the wall down."

With his help, Catherine begins bashing at the imagined wall but sees little effect. Then she starts to notice the odd small crack, then a brick or two falling away, and finally the wall crumbles and Catherine can see her sister at last.

"Caroline!"

Having said the word out loud, Logan starts at the unexpected declaration and can only hope that Catherine has found her sister. But he daren't ask, doesn't want to break his wife's concentration.

In her mind, Catherine walks tentatively towards her sister, lying quite still in a plain white room.

"Caroline, I'm here," Catherine tells her sister, putting a hand to Caroline's hair. "Please open your eyes, let me know you can hear me."

But Caroline lays still and silent, then a voice seems to echo in the room.

"I knew you would find me," Caroline's disembodied voice tells her, though the form lying in front of Catherine still hasn't moved or opened her eyes.

"Can you tell me where you are, and are you in danger?" Catherine asks, still looking down at her sister's form expecting her mouth to move in answer – but the voice comes from all around her.

"I don't know where I am, but I am most certainly in danger," Caroline declares. "I thought she was my friend, I thought she was kind and caring, but I couldn't have been more wrong."

The voice seems to be fading and Catherine grips Neil's hand more tightly, hoping to draw on his strength and ability to hold the tenuous connection to her sister. "Concentrate, Caroline – do you know her name – is she the one holding you?"

"Yes..." a faint voice echoes off the white walls, "...her name is Cherish W..." But the echo has grown too faint for the surname to be heard.

"Caroline! Caroline!" Catherine calls desperately to her sister, but has to accept that their connection has been lost.

Opening her eyes, Catherine doesn't realise that she is crying and looks at Logan as though her heart has been ripped out.

Crossing to her, Logan kneels before her and draws Catherine's head onto his shoulder, holding her while she shakes with the sobs now racking her body.

"There now, let it all out and then tell me what you found out," he croons softly, one large gentle hand stroking her hair, the other holding her firmly to him.

Minutes later, and just when he thought his own heart would break with the depth of her distress, Logan feels Catherine stiffen in his arms then pull herself upright.

"This won't help Caroline!" she states forcibly. "If I can't keep myself together my sister will pay for my weakness with her life, and I won't allow that!"

"You are not weak," Logan declares, handing her a handkerchief to wipe her eyes. "Now tell me what you were able to find out – she's obviously still alive."

"Yes..." Catherine sniffs, then blows her nose and feels better, "...but for how long I don't know. We have to get back to Travis and ask him about someone named Cherish. I couldn't hear the surname – did you?" she asks, turning to Neil with questioning eyes.

But he was shaking his head. "No, unfortunately not – though I thought it sounded like it began with a 'W'," he frowns in recollection.

"Yes, me too," Catherine agrees. "Maybe that will be enough to look her up – or maybe Travis will know who she is."

Accompanying Catherine and Logan back to the hotel; Neil contemplates ways he might be able to help find the arsonist responsible for the two blazes that have cost so many lives.

The car park has cleared, somewhat, since they left it earlier that morning. Catherine supposes they've gone in search of more gruesome details to fill the 'news' slots on both television and in the newspapers.

Walking into the main foyer, Catherine can see that the activity there has lessened also and walks to the reception desk. "We're going up to the penthouse..." she informs the receptionist, "...would you inform Mr Travis that we're bringing a guest with us – Mr Neil Farraday."

"Yes, Miss Catherine," the young woman nods.

Moving to the penthouse lift, Neil reaches out to press the button and nothing happens. Frowning, he tries again. "I don't think this is working..."

Chuckling, Catherine punches a few numbers in on the keypad above the lift button then presses it again and it lights up. "Just a code for privacy," she smiles over at Neil.

"Didn't think..." he nods in understanding.

"It stops confused guests from using the wrong lift and ending up in the penthouse," Logan explains.

When the lift doors open at the penthouse, Travis is waiting, anxious for news.

"Catherine, Logan, and Mr Farraday..." Travis greets them, reigning in the flood of questions that he is eager to ask, "...did you find anything useful?

Moving to lay a hand on Travis' arm, Catherine looks up into his fiercely worried eyes, "Not a lot, I'm afraid. But we did make contact with Caroline," she smiles encouragingly.

Sitting on the two large settees, the group settle themselves for what is sure be a difficult discussion.

"You did...and what happened...do you know where she is...?" Travis almost gets to his feet again, but Catherine puts a hand on his arm to restrain him.

"No, not exactly..." Catherine hesitates. "But we do know that Caroline is being held against her will, and before we lost contact she managed to give us a name."

She doesn't know why, but Catherine feels a deep dread at the thought of giving Travis this part of the information.

"Does the name, Cherish, mean anything to you...?" she asks softly.

Paling instantly, Travis loses his ability to speak for a moment and Neil adds, "Her surname may begin with a 'W' – we couldn't make it out; that is when the link was broken."

"Cherish Wade..." Travis' voice is little more than a whisper.

"You do know her!" Catherine states, her tone almost accusatory.

"Catherine..." Logan warns, but Travis cuts him off.

"No, Catherine is right to be angry...this is entirely my fault," Travis admits, leaning forward to cup his head in his hands.

The three spectators cast speculating glances between them, then turn to look at Travis as he gets to his feet and moves to the telephone.

"Just give me a moment then, hopefully, I'll be able to explain," he tells them vaguely.

"What the hell?!" Catherine whispers angrily to Logan, flinging a hand out in Travis' direction.

"Just be patient..." Logan puts a finger to his lips in warning, "...give Travis a chance to explain before you fly off the handle without real cause."

Firming her lips, Catherine sits back on the settee, but her spine remains stiff and her shoulders are squared to do battle.

"I'm sorry...I just needed to check to be sure," Travis tells them wearily as he retakes his seat.

For what seems like endless minutes, Travis sits contemplating the floor, his mind trying to straighten out the information he's just been given.

"Cherish Wade was my first real love," Travis admits, and hears Catherine's sharply drawn in breathe.

"We were so young, but I have no doubt that we would have married had things not gone so terribly wrong," he admits sadly.

"Cherish was the kindest, loveliest young woman you could ever wish to meet. We courted faithfully, never even looking at other prospective partners – we only saw each other," he smiles sadly.

"Doesn't sound like the same woman who is holding my sister," Catherine sneers sceptically. "You sure you're not remembering what you wanted her to be like, rather than what she actually was?!"

"Maybe. Maybe." Travis shakes his head, trying to think through the fog clouding his brain. "No...Cherish was lovely, was kind and was not the sort of woman to start fires and kill people," he states more firmly, then appears to deflate as the memories flood back.

"Her parents had begun to notice changes in her behaviour – she became fearful, paranoid, couldn't distinguish reality from fantasy and used to talk to someone who wasn't really there," Travis recalls sadly.

"Sounds like classic schizophrenia," Catherine frowns, not liking the sound of her sister's captor. "What happened to her?"

Nodding, Travis looks over at the woman who is identical in almost every way to his missing wife – just looking at her makes his heart clutch painfully.

Putting a hand to his ravaged cheek, Travis continues, "Cherish was indeed diagnosed as schizophrenic – but there were other psychological complications that made treating her precarious at best and sometimes not possible at all."

"So why haven't we heard of this woman before?" Catherine asks, hardening herself against Cherish, not wanting to feel pity for her. *I need to stay focused on getting Caroline away from her, not let myself get sidetracked by my feelings!*

"Because she's been hospitalised for the last 18 years," Travis sighs heavily. "But recently, Cherish was released having been reviewed by the doctors caring for her. They believed her condition to be under control, had gradually given her more and more responsibility for her own medications and self cares – she was apparently doing very well."

"Well, that's no longer the case," Catherine blue eyes glitter with outage. "So what did they suggest – are they coming to take her back?"

Travis looks nonplussed when his eyes flick up to Catherine, "Take her back...?"

"The doctors – surely they won't leave her to run amok, killing people willy-nilly!" No longer able to sit, Catherine gets to her feet her arms flaying wildly. "Don't they have procedures for just this sort of eventuality – I can't believe this is the first time something like this has happened?!"

"I told them the possibilities; but as they said, we can't absolutely accuse Cherish as we have no proof that she is even involved," Travis explains.

"No proof...!"

Logan turns to Catherine and takes her hand, pulling her gently to sit on the arm of the settee. "Travis is right, we can't go to the police and say that you and Neil had some kind of mental telepathy chat with Caroline and that she told you her captor's name – they'd throw us all in the bloody loony bin!"

Then Logan turns to Travis looking shamefaced, "Sorry...I didn't mean anything..."

Holding up a hand palm outwards, Travis shakes his head and says, "It's how most people see schizophrenia, but it isn't an accurate view for the most part."

"Ok, if we can't convince anyone that Cherish Wade has taken Caroline, then we have to find her ourselves and bring my sister home," Catherine states firmly.

Knowing his sister-in-law's extraordinary brainpower and computer skills, Travis feels heartened at this thought. But also wonders about the 'other' options.

"You say you made contact with Caroline..." he begins cautiously, "...does that mean that you might be able to do so again?"

Looking to each of his guests in turn, Travis can only hope that this might at least give him news of Caroline's wellbeing.

"We might get a stronger link now that we're in Caroline's own home," Neil suggests tentatively, leaning forward to look across Logan to Catherine.

"Jesus! I hate all this woowoo crap – but if it can help find Caroline we'll give it another go," Catherine agrees reluctantly.

Neil gets to his feet then turns a quizzical brow towards the sound of a baby crying.

"Our daughters," Travis informs him. "We have twin girls, Leanne and Sara. I think they've begun to sense that something is wrong — Caroline never goes this long without seeing them."

"Do you want me to help you with them," Catherine offers.

But Travis is keen to get news of Caroline, and Catherine is his only avenue for this.

"No, I'll ring down for one of the girls — between us we'll be able to manage," he asserts hopefully. "I'd rather you try to find out more about Caroline, if you wouldn't mind."

Turning to Neil, Catherine closes her eyes and lets out a long sigh. "Come on then, we'll use the bedroom to see if it helps."

"I'm going to contact Emma..." Logan informs the room, drawing out his mobile as he does so, "...we need all the help we can get on this and Emma would want us to ask her."

Hesitating, not wanting to disturb her colleague and friend's family weekend, Catherine finally nods in agreement then crosses to Caroline's bedroom with Neil close behind her.

CHAPTER SIX

By the time they arrive back at Lakelands, Logan and Catherine feel tired, hungry and full of dismay.

The session with Neil in the penthouse hadn't gone well; even surrounded by lots of Caroline's personal possessions, and in her own bedroom, Catherine hadn't been able to make any kind of a link with her sister.

"I don't know anything about such things..." Henry frowns over the kitchen table at his son and daughter-in-law, "...but I imagine stress has a lot to do with the mind's ability to do these things. Perhaps it will happen when you aren't trying so hard, hey?"

I love that you want to comfort me, but this is my sister's life we're talking about, not the name of some person or place that's on the tip of my tongue just out of reach. I have to find her. I have to!

"I'm sure you're right," Catherine smiles weakly, taking another small forkful of the lovely dinner that Henry and Linda have jointly prepared.

"Have you been in touch with your Inspector friend: Mr Harper?" Linda asks cautiously.

"Frank? No, he deals with homicide not missing persons," Catherine answers distractedly.

Frowning, Logan says, "But this is homicide — the arson attacks have taken many lives."

"Yes..." Catherine agrees, stretching the word out in contemplation, "...but Caroline has been listed as a missing person and no connection can be proved between her disappearance and the arson cases."

Pouring a glass of water and filling Catherine's empty glass, Logan shakes his head, "I don't think Frank would see it that way — especially not when we tell him about the link you made with Caroline."

Hardly daring to hope, Catherine looks at him doubtfully then lays her knife and fork down.

"I'll give him a call," she says, and looks from one worried face to another before leaving the room.

Surprising everyone, Linda lays down her cutlery and pushes the half eaten meal away from her. "If you wouldn't see it as interfering, I'd like to help find Caroline. I believe I can help give you an idea of the arsonist's frame of mind and maybe even where she might strike again or be holding Caroline.”

Looking stunned and then swiftly grateful, Logan shakes his head, “I should have remembered; you’re a trained Psychologist! Any help would be a boon, I’m sure Catherine will be very glad of it.”

“And Emma...” Henry asks, frowning quizzically, “...will she be helping Catherine?”

Nodding decisively, Logan finishes his meal and sits back in his chair giving his stomach a satisfied rub. “She’s on her way back as we speak. It’s been all over the news so Emma was already aware of the devastating fires – once I told her about Caroline I couldn’t have kept her away if I’d wanted to!”

Pursing her lips and nodding with satisfaction, Linda says, “Just so. Emma is a caring sort, not much she wouldn’t do for Catherine.”

“That goes both ways,” Logan nods in agreement. “They might go at each other hammer and tongue sometimes, but they’ve got the greatest respect and regard for each other too.”

“I’ll just set the kitchen to rights then I’ll go up and see what I can do,” Linda suggest, pushing her chair back and making to clear the table.

"No need for that..." Henry waves her away, "...we can take care of this – you go and help Catherine."

With a smile of thanks, Linda does as she's told and leaves the two men to clear away.

Going up to Catherine's office, Linda gives a tentative knock then enters the room cautiously. "I was wondering if you might be able to use my psychology background in any way. I might be able to pick up some indicators from the information you already have," she offers quietly.

"Bloody hell! I didn't even think of that – what an idiot!" Catherine berates herself, shaking her head in disgust.

Chuckling softly, Linda walks to Catherine's side.

"Logan said the same," she smiles, not in the least offended at being overlooked. "If I could take a look at the information you have..."

Jumping to her feet, Catherine goes through the pictures pinned with magnets to the whiteboards and explains, "I took these because it's said that some perpetrators like to return to the scene of their crime – some kind of perverted enjoyment in seeing the damage and distress they've caused."

Seeing Linda nod in agreement, Catherine continues, "I downloaded these from police records – they show how all the exits to the school had been sealed in one way or another and if you look over here, you can see that the cinema exits were similarly sealed off."

Linda doesn't balk at looking at the shocking photos, but concentrates her mind objectively.

"I printed these off of a newsreel that I hacked into – it shows some footage taken on mobile phones not long after the cinema blaze took hold so could have the perpetrator on them," Catherine purses her lips and looks at Linda hopefully.

"Very possible," Linda agrees.

"These are lists of people who died in the fires – one for the school victims and this one for the cinema victims, though it needs updating," Catherine frowns sadly. "Another two people have died today."

"Ok, and what have you found out about Cherish Wade – you told us that she has been released from the psychiatric unit, but have you any information that she was in the area at the time of the fires?" Linda asks, looking at Catherine with unemotional eyes.

"No, nothing," Catherine sighs heavily. "We only have what I got from Caroline but I think it's a very strong lead!"

Nodding, Linda moves back to the beginning of the photo's and begins to look at them more closely. "They don't seem to have made any attempt at sealing the ground floor windows of the school," she observes, then moves to look at the cinema photos. "And here..." Linda points to photos of the cinema windows, "...no sign of restraint on these windows either."

Frowning, Catherine asks, "So, what do you get from that...are you saying that the arsonist didn't necessarily want to kill everyone?"

"Oh no, not at all..." Linda shakes her head, her mouth pulling into a wry smile, "...but I think they wanted more than mere death – they wanted to witness the struggle for life."

"They..."

Unable to get her head round such a diabolical idea, Catherine falls silent.

"Setting a fire in this way, the arsonist was intending to take as many lives as possible..." Linda explains, "...but it all takes place inside the building, away from their field of vision. But leave even the minutest hope of survival and there's every possibility that some of the victims will find it and try to escape. That would have made a very satisfying spectacle to someone capable of carrying out this kind of murder."

"Jesus!" Catherine is stunned to think that anyone could be that calculating...but then remembers Edwards. Her mother's murderer had tortured her in the most awful ways possible and had come prepared with his own set of 'instruments'. He'd apparently stalked his victims, building up a timetable of their movements, their lifestyle and availability.

That last had been a real shocker when Edwards' possessions had been seized. As well as designs for improved instruments of torture, he had notebooks full of observations he'd carried out on various women. If he couldn't ensure a window of at least 4 hours in the victim's home he would move on to someone else.

He actually put that, must be available for at least 4 hours – the sick bastard wanted to ensure he had time to really enjoy himself!

"Catherine...?" Linda Baines had turned in time to see the memories cause Catherine to pale visibly and her hands are shaking badly.

"He wanted to make sure that it was worth his while," Catherine recalls aloud. "If he was going to go to all that trouble, he wanted his just reward..."

"Are we still talking about the arsonist?" Linda asks gently, putting a comforting hand to Catherine's arm.

"No...yes...I mean... It's all the same, isn't it? Edwards, this arsonist, they both wanted some kind of payback for something they see as having been done against them," Catherine speculates.

"If these fires are being set by Cherish Wade - and I do believe they are..." Catherine attests firmly, her blue eyes steely as they regard the woman standing alongside her, "...then maybe she is punishing Travis for something she believes he did to her. If we can work out what that was, maybe we can start to see where she's going with this, what her end game is."

"Yes...only, for now I think you need to run the two investigations side by side," Linda suggests. "There doesn't appear to be any proof that Cherish Wade was involved in setting the fires — that could have been a happenstance that she took advantage of to get to Caroline; if indeed that was her original goal," Linda frowns thoughtfully. "I just wish I could get my hands on her medical notes..."

"You can," Catherine smiles, snapping out of her lugubrious thoughts. "I've got them up right now — I can print them off for you."

Jaw dropping, Linda gapes after her as Catherine crosses back to her desk and does what she does best. Working on her laptop, she has hacked into Cherish Wade's medical records to get some background information on the woman.

But if a trained Psychologist were to look these over I'm sure they'd find things I wouldn't even think to look for, might make connections that wouldn't be evident to a lay person like me.

"There's quite a bit of them," Catherine warns. "I already downloaded the medical files from her GP; which are quite extensive from the time Wade began exhibiting symptoms that were eventually diagnosed as schizophrenia – I'll print those off first."

Seconds later the printer begins spewing forth pages and Catherine goes back to the psychiatric notes from the Sanatorium that she had been reading prior to Linda coming in.

"It states that she was very combative and confrontational on admission and for a couple of months thereafter," Catherine muses out loud. "And she asked for Travis repeatedly."

Frowning, Catherine considers this and looks more carefully at the notations. "Wade never once asked for her parents – that's kind of odd, don't you think?" she adds, looking up at Linda.

Nodding her agreement, Linda rounds the desk to stand behind Catherine and begins to read.

Wade has fallen into a Catatonic stupor – no amount of stimulation has gained even the vaguest response. Parents informed - they were asked to visit and try eliciting a response from their daughter by talking to her and playing familiar music, but this was discontinued after the first visit. Mrs Wade become very upset at the sight of her daughter in her present state and was unable to continue. No further visits envisaged.

"So they just left her there!" Catherine couldn't imagine anything worse. Her own situation, growing up in stranger's houses with pseudo siblings, had been hard to take and not something she would wish on any child, but at least she'd had times when she could get away, be by herself and block it all out.

But you didn't have the chance to do that did you? You would have been surrounded by other disturbed minds, some of them extremely vocal and maybe even violent on occasion. Hiding inside your head would have been your only escape...only you didn't come back for a very long time.

Hardening her heart lest her sympathy detract from the task in hand, Catherine gets to her feet.

Crossing to the printer she begins needlessly organising the pages as they emerge to give her hands something to do. But her mind keeps thinking back to when she had been a patient in a psychiatric unit and how her only comfort had been her own mind.

She hadn't spoken for 2 years after being forced to witness her mother's torture murder; words had become unimportant and meaningless.

But the dreams, the nightmares, they had woken her often, especially in the early days.

I still get them, only now I can stay silent when I wake. I learned that trick early on; being restrained and medicated after nightmares was a torture in itself. They may have meant well, but I had seen what happens to people who are tied to their beds and the thought of it terrified me.

"Catherine...?" Linda puts a hand to her arm in concern, the younger woman having paled and a dewy sweat shone on her brow.

"I'm fine...really." Not taking her eyes away from the pages still issuing from the printer, Catherine forces herself to breathe more deeply, to steady herself and regain her steely control.

Watching her efforts, Linda decides not to press the point but moves to the whiteboards to allow Catherine time to recompose.

"It's a pity they didn't think to take annual photographs of Cherish..." Linda observes, looking intently into the faces of the people shown in the photographs of the two arson attacks, "...we might have been able to identify her on one of these."

Grateful for the diversion, Catherine crosses to Linda's side and also looks more closely at the pictures.

And then a thought hits her. "We may not know what she looks like today but we can do a computer generated aging to give us a good idea. And we can examine these photos to see if anyone appears at both scenes – not an easy task but certainly possible."

The printer finally stops and Catherine moves to gather up the sheets of paper handing the intimidating pile to Linda. "If you could just make sure that these don't get mixed in with the GP notes I'd be grateful. It'll be the devils own job to sort them out if you do!"

Feeling a little slighted, Linda bites back a retort about being professional enough to know that without being told and satisfies herself with a curt nod instead.

Unaware of the discord, Catherine turns back to her desk and settles behind her laptop. It takes a while to find a photograph of Cherish Wade, unlike America, English schools don't produce year books and they don't keep copies of the annual school photos either.

It is by searching the Sheriton Police Department's records that she finds a photograph of Cherish along with a report concerning actual bodily harm committed against one Travis Lovett, 18 years ago.

"Well, fuck a duck!" Catherine exclaims in surprise. "So that's how Travis got his injuries – that bloody lunatic glassed him!"

"What?" Linda turns from the pictures she's been studying and crosses quickly to Catherine's side.

"Jesus, she made a right mess of his face," Catherine grimaces at the photographs of Travis' injuries. "She apparently rammed a broken wine glass into his face repeatedly, he was lucky to keep the eye."

<u>CHAPTER SEVEN</u>

Lying in the warm embrace of her husband's arms, Catherine once again thanks her lucky stars that they found each other.

"Did you ever have second thoughts about me after I told you that I'd been a patient in a loony bin?" she asks, her fingers playing idly with the hairs on Logan's bare chest.

They had discussed the attack on Travis the night before with Henry and Linda, and she had wondered then if they secretly worried that she might do something just as terrible at some slight provocation.

Tightening his arm around her shoulders, Logan tries to look down at her but Catherine has her face buried in his chest.

"No I bloody didn't! And you are nothing like Cherish Wade," he states firmly, managing to get a hand under her chin to tip her face up to look at him. "The poor woman is sick – schizophrenia is eminently treatable, though Travis did mention other mental health complications that made that difficult. But even so, your hospitalisation was nothing like Ms Wade's."

Not replying immediately, Catherine lays her head back on his chest and moves further into his side. "I know where she went when she disappeared into her head," she murmurs softly. "Sometimes the world becomes too vivid, too painful to live in and it's easier just to shrink back into the shadows, to find a safe place where no one can hurt you, not ever again."

Remembering the time in Edwards' kitchen when Catherine had seemed to do just that, Logan again tightens his arms about her and kisses the top of her head.

"I will never let anyone harm you; you or the boys," Logan promises, his low oath rumbling in her ears. "I love you more than life, and nothing will ever tear us apart."

Feeling a warm tear run down into the hairs of his chest, Logan can only hope that she believes him. He knows what a troubled soul Catherine is, but he also knows that she has a great capacity to care about others more than herself; even if she isn't particularly good at showing it.

When Emma arrives, Catherine is overjoyed but you would never know it from the greeting she gives.

Glancing up from her desk as the door opens, she looks at Emma and simply says, "Get the coffee on whilst you're up, then I've got a couple of jobs for you to do."

"It's good to see you, too," Emma chuckles, moving to the mugs and preparing to make coffee. "If I didn't know better, I'd say you've missed me. But then my mother always said I look for the best in any situation."

"Ha ha," Catherine smirks, then her lips pull into a genuine smile. "I missed your coffee – I always make it too strong."

Passing her a mug of fresh coffee, Emma picks up the empty mug sitting on Catherine's desk and takes it to the small sink.

"I've kept up to date with the arson attacks," she tells Catherine while rinsing the mug out. "Do we have any concrete leads? Or any leads," Emma asks, crossing the room to her desk.

Picking up her mug of coffee, Catherine holds it between her hands, looking down into it contemplatively. "More than we usually do – though nothing concrete."

After getting a brief update about Cherish Wade, her previous involvement with Travis, and Linda's view on the arson attacks, Emma moves on to the other case they're looking at.

"And Caroline – have we got any leads as to where she is?" Emma asks, her voice all business so as not to become emotional, believing that wouldn't do anyone any good.

"No – that's the first job I want you to do." Catherine leans back in her seat regarding Emma across the room, knowing that she is as logical and methodical as she is herself. "We've already checked out Wade's parent's old address and crossed it off the list. They've been dead around 5 years; died within a year of each other," Catherine observes with a frown. "Funny how couples often do that," she muses quietly.

"So what happened to the house – has it been sold?" Emma asks.

"Yes. Some relative or other saw to it and the proceeds were divvied up according to the will. Which means Ms Wade is not short of funds," Catherine adds with a quirked up brow.

Emma sits forward in her chair considering, "Do we know how much, and have you accessed her bank account to follow the money?"

"No and no," Catherine sighs loudly. "She closed the bloody account the minute she was released – Christ knows where she's stashed it, I've checked all the local banks but found nothing."

Nodding, Emma sips her coffee, turning numerous thoughts over in her mind. "Are Frank and Sloane on board?" she asks eventually.

Raising her brow even higher, Catherine's eyes go wide, "You and Sloane not all lovey-dovey on the phone while you've been away? Or is there trouble in paradise again?"

Letting out a disgusted growl, Emma shoves to her feet and flicks a dismissive hand towards Catherine. "Don't even go there! Bloody man!"

Used to the on again, off again, relationship between Emma and Sloane, Catherine merely chuckles then puts her coffee mug down and joins her friend at the whiteboards.

"You ok?" she asks dutifully.

"I'm fine," Emma replies, and actually does seem to be alright. "I think we're both too set in our ways to give in easy to the restrictions a grown-up relationship puts on you. And I don't like being told what to do," she adds tellingly.

Making a noncommittal noise in her throat, Catherine declines to make any comment. "I called Frank first thing this morning – he's part of a large team that's been put together to catch the arsonist. He and Sloane will be coming round some time before lunch – is that going to be a problem?"

Lifting her chin a full inch, Emma continues to look at the whiteboards and says, "Not for me."

Making the same non committal sound at the back of her throat, Catherine begins to think the day ahead could get interesting.

Then, just as she's about to speak, Emma beats her to it and asks, "How's Adrianne and Tom doing – they must be distraught with Caroline going missing?"

Blushing, knowing that she isn't looking forward to facing her father later this afternoon, Catherine grimaces.

"We've managed to keep that bit of news away from Adrianne so far, but my dad wasn't best pleased when he found out. Said I should have told him as soon as I knew 'his daughter' was missing," Catherine frowns uncomfortably.

Not, 'you should have told me when your sister went missing', oh no, it had been 'my daughter'. But then, I suppose Caroline has been his daughter for a lot longer than she's been my sister. But I wonder if he would have said it quite that possessively if it had been me that had gone missing? Would he even have thought 'my daughter' had it been me?

Giving her head an annoyed shake, Catherine determinedly pulls herself out of her useless reverie.

But Emma hasn't missed the hurt inflection in her friend's voice, and turns to look at Catherine, finding nothing but a look of detached concentration on her face.

"I'm sure your dad didn't mean anything by it," she assures her.

But Catherine has pulled the blinds down over her expression and stubbornly refuses to be drawn. "Caroline is the most important focus right now. If you do a search for Wade you might find something for us to work on – at the moment, we haven't got a bloody thing!"

She doesn't know why, but Catherine hasn't told Emma about her failed attempts at contacting her sister using their unique connection. She had felt like she'd let her sister down and still feels guilty over it.

"Alright, I'll get right on it," Emma smiles, touching a hand to Catherine's arm as she passes by her.

"I'm going to search these pictures, see if I can find a face that appears at both crime scenes," Catherine sighs, and crosses back to her desk. "And I'll set the aging programme to work to get an up to date facial on Wade."

Emma's head turns abruptly, "Where did you get a photo of Wade from? Surely Travis didn't have one to give you?"

"I didn't ask him," Catherine bristles angrily. "But if he has he'd better not let me know about it!"

"So, where did you get it from?" Emma persists.

"Police files. They had photos from her arrest after the assault she carried out on Travis," Catherine explains.

"It's hard to believe that a young woman, supposedly in love with Travis, did that awful thing to his beautiful face," Emma reflects soulfully.

"Yeah, just goes to show, you can't trust anyone!"

Concerned at Catherine's downturn in mood, Emma decides to change the subject. "Adrianne still hasn't popped yet, then? I mean, you didn't actually say..."

"No, Robert is all but pulling his hair out waiting and Adrianne is so big she bounces off everything like a pinball," Catherine chuckles, her smile returning.

"Poor Adrianne," Emma sympathises. Then surprises Catherine by saying, "Sloane wants kids."

"What?!"

Catherine is gaping over at Emma, stunned by the complete non sequitur.

"That's what we argued about..." Emma states as she walks over to Catherine's desk, "...he wants kids!"

Not at all sure what to say, Catherine stares up at Emma feeling like she's just had the solid floor jerked out from under her.

"I.I...what did you say...?"

"I told him that having kids is not something you just do," Emma replies, her brown eyes molten with the pent up anger she has managed to suppress thus far. But it is out now and her eyes are ablaze as she stands with hands on hips looking at Catherine.

"No, no you're right. But why now," Catherine asks curiously.

"Ha! That's what I said!" Emma shoots out an arm and points an accusing finger at Catherine. "See, even you think it's a crazy idea. I asked him, why now, why are you suddenly desperate for children?!"

I know I'm going to regret this, but I can't not ask... "And what did he say?"

"What did he say? What did he say?" Emma screeches, her voice going higher with the repeating. "I'll tell you what that bloody man said – 'we're both getting on a bit, and if we want kids we ought to get on with it'."

Catherine wants to laugh, but thinks better of it.

What an idiot! He not only demands children but insults her in the process. Men!

"Err...did he say anything about getting married first, or...?"

Letting out a derisive laugh, Emma's eyes go round, her brows lifting comically. "Oh yes, that did get a mention." And Emma slowly lets out a long drawn out breathe to calm herself. "When I told him that I wouldn't be having children any time soon, he asked me why. And when I told him that, old fashioned as it might be I believe in being married first, he said 'ok, if that's what you want'."

With her mouth gaping and her hands held palms up and out in front of her, Emma looks at Catherine with an expression that says, 'can you believe that!'

"Oh, so he does want to marry you at least," Catherine blows out a relieved breathe. Then gulps and sits back into her seat when Emma takes a long step forward to glare hotly down at her.

"Great! So you think I should be grateful that he's willing to marry me, especially as I'm obviously knocking on a bit!"

Beginning to panic, not used to dealing with people and their emotions, Catherine tries to think of something placatory to say but her usually high functioning brain fails her. And so she falls back on her old reliable tack of good old fashioned honesty.

"What I think doesn't really matter, does it?" Catherine meets Emma's glaring eyes unwaveringly. "But, as you're asking, I personally think you need your head read for even going out with the jerk – let alone considering tying yourself to the man for life!"

Looking blank for a second, Emma then begins to nod her head in agreement, and Catherine surreptitiously sighs with relief. "I really do, don't I?! That bloody man has been nothing but trouble since the day I met him. He's always banging on about our work and the laws we're breaking – yet he and Frank have found our skills useful more than once!"

Deciding not to say anything, Catherine just waits as Emma builds another head of steam.

"I mean, it's not like we use the information we get for our own profit!" Then she tilts her head to one side and her shoulders drop, "Ok, we do, but only to help us find missing people or to help a client in some way. I mean, we don't hack banks or stock reports for our own financial gain – but we could if we were so inclined, but we're not!"

Watching Emma pace around the office, her hands and arms flailing around as her temper rises, Catherine has to admire her friend's depth of feeling and her ability to vocalise it.

"You know what..." Catherine shakes her head then smiles when Emma finally runs out of steam, "...that is some impressive temper you have there. I couldn't have said all that any better myself!"

Looking sideways at Catherine and narrowing her eyes suspiciously, Emma sees that she is being serious. "I always have had a good temper – my mother said it would land me in trouble one day."

"Was she right?" Catherine asks with a grin.

And with an answering grin, Emma says, "Frequently!"

Letting out a low growl, Emma gives herself an all over shake as if shrugging off the black mood.

"Right, now that I've got that out of my system I'll get back to business." And crossing to her desk, Emma sits down behind her laptop and begins tapping keys like nothing has happened.

Deciding not to think about the fact that 'lover-boy' and his boss are due to make an appearance in a couple of hours, Catherine also gets back to the work of finding an arsonist and her sister.

CHAPTER EIGHT

Dressing carefully, Cherish Wade puts the finishing touches to her perfect make-up then moves to stand in front of the full length mirror in her room.

Smoothing steady hands over her hips she admires the way the midnight blue dress slides over them, highlighting their slimness. Then she turns a foot, this way and that, loving the matching stiletto heels that accentuate the length of her toned calves.

Yes, Travis has always loved my legs and I've worked hard to make the best of them. Being cooped up for so long allowed my muscles to slacken, but I think they're looking much better now.

The plain girl that Travis fell in love with has blossomed with the clever use of make-up and a professional hairdo.

Her dull brown hair is now shining with health and curves under her chin in a smooth bob.

Smiling at her reflection, Cherish nods her head in imaginary greeting and says, "Hello Travis, how lovely to see you again." Then she chuckles girlishly at an imagined reply and says, "Thank you, you always were a gentleman. I've missed you, Travis, how about a drink over dinner if you have the time?"

And of course he'll say yes because he really is too much of a gentleman to refuse me. Then it will be me and Travis, just as it was always meant to be...

At the back of a large sliding bookcase in the sitting room is a secret room and hidden within lies Caroline, drugged but still very much alive.

"Back soon, sweetie..." Cherish calls after picking up her purse from the settee, "...I won't give Travis your love, he'll be too busy enjoying mine."

With a hideous laugh, Cherish leaves the house she is renting just 150 yards from The Lovett Hotel, and smiles at the thought of seeing Travis again.

As she passes the burned out cinema her smile widens and puts a spring in her step. *This really is working out better than I planned, and no one is any the wiser. I can walk out with my head held high and absolutely nobody suspects that it was me!*

'Better be careful' the voice in her head whispers softly, 'we don't want to get caught now. No, that wouldn't do at all, we have a lot to do...no, that wouldn't do at all.'

"Shut up!" Cherish snaps out loud, causing a passer-by to turn quickly to look at her. Then she whispers quietly, "Just stay quiet or we'll both get caught and then where will we be?"

The voice falls silent and Cherish walks on, her face a mask of serenity, her emotions held in check.

The lights from the hotel are bright and welcoming, the driveway lit by old fashioned lampposts dotted amongst the shrubs and lawns.

"I've always loved this place..." Cherish recalls dreamily, "...we used to spend hours walking together in the rear gardens."

Stepping through the entrance doors into the foyer, Cherish stops at the reception desk to ask if there are any vacancies for dinner. "I'm sorry I didn't book earlier, I was expecting company and they didn't let me know they wouldn't be coming until the last moment," Cherish smiles charmingly.

"Not to worry, madam," the receptionist returns her smile and looks at the restaurant bookings on her computer. "Yes, we have a small table free – may I take your name please?"

"Cherish Wade."

"Ok, Ms Wade, I've booked that for you - if you follow the signs for the restaurant our maître d' will seat you as soon as you are ready. Enjoy your meal."

Deciding to have a glass of wine in the lounge first, Cherish makes her way to the bar and places her order with great satisfaction. Many heads have turned in her direction, though she studiously pays them no attention.

Thanking the barman, flashing him her most charming smile, Cherish takes her wine and sits at a vacant table facing the outer doors.

Maybe I'll get lucky and see Travis going about his business. It would be lovely to have dinner with him, he is always so attentive. I'm so lucky to have him.

But after spending an hour sipping her wine, Cherish feels she must go into dinner or risk losing her table.

It's getting late to be working, but Catherine is determined to put in another couple of hours. The twins are both down for the night and Emma has gone back to the gatehouse.

Pouring another mug of coffee, she takes it back to her desk and looks at the photographs that she's been studying all afternoon.

"I'm missing something. There has to be a face in the crowd – even Linda agreed it's more than likely the arsonist was watching both fires and revisited the crime scene afterwards."

"Talking to yourself...?" Logan asks with a wry smile. "Here, take five minutes off to enjoy this."

Taking the wine glass, Catherine sits back in her seat to look up at her husband. "What is the point of having a supposedly brilliant mind if I can't do something as basic as finding my sister?"

"If it were that 'basic' the police would already have found Caroline and returned her home," Logan frowns, pulling up a chair to sit opposite her.

"I can't think straight, Logan," Catherine admits quietly. "My brain is scrambled and my logic just isn't logical anymore. I don't know how to deal with this?"

Knowing that for Catherine to admit as much she must be truly struggling, Logan begins to untangle the knots in her thinking in an unhurried, chatty kind of a way.

"Tell me what you've been doing – just list the steps without going into too much detail for now," he smiles, relaxed back in his chair like he hasn't a care in the world.

"Ok," Catherine frowns over at him suspiciously, but soon relaxes once she begins to think through the process. "Well, I downloaded some video footage of both fires from a news site – printed off a few photos from them," and she points to one of the whiteboards with the photos pinned to it with coloured magnets.

"I read the police and fire departments reports on both fires," she says quickly, having deliberately not used the words 'hacked into' so as not to raise his ire. "So we know for sure that the two are connected.

"You've been looking for previous arson attacks within a 50 mile radius of Sheriton, and Emma has been trying to find Cherish Wade," she frowns thoughtfully. "I got a photo of her from the police report of the assault on Travis – then I ran an aging programme that I've managed to tweak, and it came up with a face that should be something like what Wade looks like today."

Again she points to one of the whiteboards and Logan is stunned to see a face he recognises.

"I know her!" he gasps, getting quickly to his feet to cross the room and stare into the eyes of a suspected murderer.

Following just as quickly, Catherine stands at his side staring from the photo to Logan and back again. "How? Did she buy property from you recently? Are you still in touch with her?"

"No. Yes. Just give me a second to think," Logan demands, holding up a staying hand to silence his wife.

"I was in our Sheriton estate agency, just going over a few possible development properties I'm interested in, when she came in looking for somewhere to rent or buy," he recalls, his brows drawn together in deep concentration.

"I don't know where she got the money, considering she's been locked up for the last 18 years, but she wasn't interested in our mortgage services," he remembers clearly. "She didn't mind renting if the property was suitable, but wanted to buy outright if possible – a cash purchase, she said."

Looking at each other, Catherine and Logan mull over what that could mean.

"The money came from her parents – they're dead and the house was sold, plus they had a decent amount of money set aside that she inherited exclusively," Catherine tells him, her sigh one of contemplation rather than dejection. And Logan can see the cogs of her mind beginning to turn more smoothly.

"Can you write down the areas she was interested in living, and any contact details you have," she asks Logan hopefully.

"I didn't deal with her myself – Sean went through everything with her and took down her details." Looking at his watch, Logan decides to give him a call. "It's only

8:30, he won't mind if I call him to ask if he remembers her."

And while Catherine goes back to her laptop, Logan gets out his mobile to contact his manager.

By the time he gets off the phone the printer is in motion and Catherine crosses the room to take out the sheet of paper now sitting in its tray.

"He remembers her..." Logan informs Catherine as she walks back to her desk "...but he can't remember her details off the top of his head, unfortunately."

"Don't worry about it..." she smiles, shutting down her laptop and moving to the whiteboard with Wade's picture on it, "...I've got them." And she holds up the sheet of paper then takes down the aged photo of Wade.

"Hold it!" Logan steps in front of her, effectively using his body to block Catherine's exit. "What do you mean...you've got them?"

She'd been hoping to skip out quickly, diverting his attention with a trip to Sheriton – but his mind is as sharp as hers, it seems.

"I've got them," she repeats blithely. "I just printed them off. Now, we need to go to The Lovett – I want to show this photo around in case anyone can recognise her from it."

But when she moves to get past him, Logan just moves his bulk sideways to cut her off. "How?"

Just one word, but he made it sound so damned threatening somehow.

"Look, we needed the information and I didn't see how Sean was going to remember a client's details, just like that, when he deals with so many people," Catherine huffs, then puts both hands to the flat of his hard abdomen and gives Logan an annoyed push.

He doesn't even teeter, not a step back or even a sway. Logan plays rugby against men who are giants compared to her and Catherine has to admit defeat.

"Ok, damn it! I hacked your system and got the details..." she stares up at him defiantly, "...but you knew that, so why make me say it?!"

"Yes, I knew that – my point is, you should have asked," Logan replies in a voice so annoyingly reasonable that it gets Catherine's hackles rising.

Even stretching herself up to her full and considerable height, Catherine doesn't come close to looking Logan in the eyes. But her blue eyes are glinting ferociously up at his all the same.

"Why – you already know that's what I do, it's who I am and you can't change me," she tells him, with a finger jabbing into his chest.

"I know who you are and what you do and I wouldn't change a single thing about you," Logan tells her, his voice dangerously low his gaze hot and penetrating. "But this is who I am..."

Before she can even consider what he's about to do, Logan pulls her into his arms and kisses her senseless. His lips are not gentle, his hands roving over her body are not asking but taking, and when he pushes her up against the office wall she can feel the hard length of him pulsing against her abdomen.

He isn't forcing himself on her, but Catherine really has no choice but to answer his need. Her body is responding to him in every way possible, Logan is her mate, the other half of her soul, and once his needs are made clear her only instinct is to satisfy them and he hers.

I need to feel you...I can't get close enough...just...oh god, yes, yes...

"This is who I am," Logan repeats, his large hands shucking her up the wall and pulling her legs around his waist, and then he plunges into her. Deep and forceful, his penetration is possessive, all consuming and insanely thrilling.

Crying out with an animal lust that is primeval, Catherine opens herself up to him gladly.

Mine! Always mine!

Clawing, pounding, biting, plunging, squeezing, gasping, their minds have nothing to do with what their bodies are doing now. All thought has vanished to be replaced by wants and needs, demands and capitulations and eventually...yes, eventually...their bodies tighten, their minds go blank and their loins send out showers of electricity to thrill every nerve ending their united body's posses.

A mass of convulsing, quivering limbs, Catherine and Logan lie naked and panting on the office floor, utterly spent and profoundly sated.

For long moments all either of them can do is to concentrate on drawing in their next lung full of air.

"Ok..." Catherine sighs breathlessly, "...next time...I'll ask..."

CHAPTER NINE

Arriving at The Lovett Hotel, Catherine and Logan first go to the reception desk and ask Jane to call up to the penthouse to let Travis know that they are in the lounge.

"I'll do that now," Jane smiles warmly. "Will you be staying for dinner – we always keep a table by for family to use?"

"Not tonight," Logan returns her smile and unknowingly causes Jane's heart to skip a couple of beats. "We're just going to enjoy a drink in the lounge."

Just as they are about to walk away, Catherine says, "Wait, could you take a look at this and tell me if you've seen her before." And she takes out the printout of the aged image of Cherish Wade, holding it out to the receptionist.

Looking carefully, Jane eventually shakes her head. "Not anyone I know, though there is something familiar about her – has she stayed here before?"

"We don't know, but we think she may be connected to my sister's disappearance so keep your eyes peeled in case she comes in."

Jane looks taken aback but nods avidly, "I'll do that, and if you'll leave that with me I'll make a copy and put it behind the desk for the rest of the staff to look at."

"Good idea," Catherine agrees, handing the picture over. "But I'd like that back as soon as you've finished – we'll be in the lounge for now."

Most people who are dining at the hotel have already gone in for their meals, and so the lounge is just comfortably populated by people enjoying a relaxing drink.

"Make mine a large white wine," Catherine tells Logan before crossing the room to seat herself at a corner table.

Not really a people person, Catherine sits studying her hands, the table menus or the coasters until Logan seats himself next to her.

"I've always enjoyed coming here..." Logan observes, "...Travis has transformed the atmosphere of the place since his parent's time."

Frowning, Catherine looks up at Logan with questioning eyes, "What was it like before?"

"Hmm, not exactly unwelcoming..." he recalls musingly, "...but very austere and aimed at the more well-to-do, I think."

"Ha! So the likes of me wouldn't have been welcome," Catherine observes correctly. "I might have had money back then, but I doubt I fitted their idea of 'well-to-do'!"

Then she laughs caustically, "I bet they would have been 'fully booked' had I walked in off the street and asked for a room. Why are people so judgemental – clothes are just clothes and hair is just hair?"

Logan's full lips pull into a wide smile as he gazes lovingly down at Catherine. "You have no vanity," he tells her. "You never have had, and money means less than nothing to you – though I noted you gave a sizeable donation to the Sheriton disaster fund."

Shrugging, Catherine picks up her wine and takes a sip, "That's what it's for, isn't it? I'm not a nurse or a doctor; I can't do anything practical to help those people, but if my money can help them to pick up the pieces of their lives then they're welcome to it."

"So, you won't leave me if my business empire goes bust," he chuckles deeply.

Taking him completely seriously, Catherine turns shocked eyes up at him. "Are you in trouble? I thought that shopping mall you transformed made you a lot of money?" she asks, then continues without giving him the time to answer. "I've told you before to put my money with yours – just use it how you want to, you don't need to ask!"

Taking her face between his large hands, Logan kisses her full on the lips not bothering who can see them. "I love you, woman!"

But Catherine is just more confused and pulls away from him, "I'm serious, Logan!"

His laughter only distresses her more, with thoughts of impending doom and believing him to be hysterical, Catherine picks up her wine and throws it in his face.

"What the..."

Thankfully the glass of wine had been only half full, and a napkin quickly soaks up the splashes on his shirt and trousers.

"Well at least it calmed you down," Catherine tells him, helping Logan to tidy himself up. "I didn't know what else to do."

"For what?" Logan asks incredulously.

"You were getting all hysterical and I-"

Catching at her busy hands, Logan stills her and waits until Catherine is looking at him. "I wasn't hysterical..." and holding up a hand to stop her from jumping in, he continues, "...and I'm not going broke."

"Then, what was all that about me not leaving you if you did?" she asks, annoyed and feeling foolish now.

"I suppose I was just admiring the fact that you love me for myself and not my bank balance," he tells her, and putting a knuckle under her chin tips her face up so that he can kiss her again. "That's a very precious gift you've given me."

Cheeks reddening and feeling awkward, Catherine doesn't quite know what to say. And so she picks up her empty wine glass instead. "For that you can fill this with something extra special," she frowns.

"It will be my pleasure," Logan grins, and taking the glass he walks tall and proud over to the bar.

At that moment, Jake, the new porter who had mistaken her for Caroline, walks over to Catherine with an anxious expression on his face.

"I'm sorry to disturb you, Miss, but it's about this picture..." and he holds out the original copy of the computer image of Cherish Wade, "...only, Jane said as you were asking if anyone knew her, or has seen her lately."

"And do you know her?" Catherine asks, sitting forward in her seat with interest.

"Yes, Miss – at least, she's the one who Miss Caroline took home," he recalls positively.

"You're absolutely sure?!" Catherine asks, getting up from her seat and clasping his hands as if not to let him escape.

Looking uncertain now, Jake tries to take a step back but Catherine holds him firmly in her grip.

"The...the hairs different..." he begins again, "...but the face is right." Then his panic gets the better of him and he pleads for forgiveness, "I'm sorry, Miss. If I'd known Miss Caroline was going to go missing... But I didn't know, did I, and what would I have been able to do...I can't drive so I couldn't have offered to take the lady home for her-"

Logan's return, with drinks in hand, cuts of the young porter's babble. "What's going on?"

"He knows Cherish Wade. He's positively identified her as the woman who Caroline gave a lift to," Catherine tells him, not taking her eyes off of Jake.

"But she couldn't have hurt her..." Jake continues hopefully, "...it must have been someone else – someone who took Miss Caroline after she'd dropped that lady off."

Now Logan is intrigued, "What makes you say that?"

"Well, sir..." the young porter chuckles nervously, "...if she'd done Miss Caroline any harm she wouldn't be daft enough to come back here – would she?"

The grip on his hands tightens painfully and Jake winces and tries to pull them free. "Back here? This woman has been back here since Caroline went missing?" Catherine demands quietly, though her voice holds a threat of tenuously bridled violence.

Looking hopefully up at Logan, Jake nods vigorously, "She's in the dining room right now...I.I saw her come in, sir."

"Then why didn't Jane recognise her?" Catherine asks, still gripping his hands tightly.

"She...she wasn't on the desk then," Jack splutters. "Jane's on the night shift tonight."

Dropping Jake's hands, Catherine's eyes go to Logan's and he can see the fierceness of her emotions.

"Wait! Just take a breath and think this through," he warns her. "If we go in there all accusing, we might frighten her off and never see her or Caroline ever again."

"So what do you suggest – should we send her a bottle of complimentary wine and hope she enjoys her meal?" Catherine sneers unattractively.

"Actually, I suggest 'we' don't do anything," Logan nods, considering his idea. "I suggest we explain everything to Travis and let him approach Ms Wade. They had a very meaningful relationship at one time – maybe he can get information from her that we wouldn't be able to."

Continuing to stare at him intently, Logan can see the moment when Catherine concedes to his idea.

"Alright, but if she leaves before he gets down here I'm going to follow her," Catherine states firmly. "So you go do your explaining to Travis and I'll sit here with Jake keeping an eye out for Wade!"

Looking at the nervous youth, Logan actually feels sorry for the boy but can't think of a reason not to agree. "I'll go up to the penthouse and explain in person." Then turning to smile reassuringly at Jake he continues, "It shouldn't take long."

Retaking her seat, Catherine looks up at Jake and says, "Sit!"

Jake does so immediately, though his small bottom perches precariously on the edge of his seat as if ready to make a run for it if needs be.

"Keep your eyes on the dining room doors..." Catherine instructs Jake, "...and if you see Wade coming out you let me know immediately. Clear?!"

"Yes, Miss," Jake actually gives her a small salute then turns to face the right way.

Not another word passes between them, so intent are they in their observations. The very expensive wine that Logan has bought for her goes untouched as Catherine contemplates her quarry.

When Travis eventually walks into the lounge, he is composed and very regal looking. His long chestnut wavy hair almost touches the shoulders of his fine suit.

"Catherine," he smiles stiffly, obviously not as relaxed as he's trying to look. Turning to the young porter, Travis addresses him directly, "Jake, you are turning out to be an invaluable member of our staff," and again he gives a stiff smile. "Would you be so kind as to ask our maitre d' exactly where Ms Wade is seated? Thank you," he adds as Jake rises immediately to do his bidding.

Pushing her untouched wine across the table, Catherine looks up at Travis and says, "You want a gulp of this first – I haven't touched it yet."

At first, Travis merely looks from Catherine to the wine and back again, then surprises her by picking the glass up and doing exactly as she'd suggested. "That was a terrible waste of one of our finest wines, if I'm not mistaken," and he turns his eyes on Logan who gives him a rueful smile and nods. "Well, let's at least hope that it does the job," and with that Travis walks over to where Jake is waiting to tell him the information he'd asked for.

Standing in the dining room doorway, Travis surveys his guests then feels a clench in his gut, so deep and painful, he's glad he'd taken up Catherine's offer of the wine.

Cherish! Oh my Lord, it is you! It really is you...

With his feet seemingly moving of their own volition, Travis finds himself standing in front of Cherish Wade even before he has made up his mind what he is going to say to her.

But Cherish takes care of that small matter. On seeing him before her, Cherish jumps to her feet and flings her arms about his neck and holds on fast. "Travis – oh my darling, Travis!"

Stunned into inaction, Travis finds himself holding her gently against his stiff body until sense finally returns.

"Cherish, perhaps we should sit down," he invites, gently peeling her off his body and moving to take a seat.

But Cherish doesn't merely sit on the opposite side of the table – she drags her chair to sit as close to Travis as is humanly possible and takes his hand with both of hers.

"Oh, Travis, I've longed to see you again," Cherish smiles, her sincerity shining bright in her deep brown eyes. "Aren't you pleased to see me?"

"Of course, Cherish..." and Travis dips his head in acknowledgement, "...but it has been a very long time, things have changed, our lives have moved on as everyone's must."

"I know, I know," Cherish tells him, but Travis can see that she doesn't know at all. "But we're still the same people, just a little older," she smiles artlessly, just as she had at 18.

With sympathy in his heart for the lovely young girl she once had been, Travis tries to let her down gently enough to still be friends. After all, this is the woman who might be holding his wife; he needs her cooperation to find Caroline.

"How are you keeping, Cherish, are you living nearby?" he asks with no more than friendly interest in his voice.

"I would like to have moved back into my parent's place, but it was sold while I.I was away," she finishes haltingly, her voice tailing off to a whisper.

Looking down into her lap, Cherish looks uncertain and Travis finds himself moved despite himself.

"But you are back now, and if you aren't living at your parents house then where?" he persists, though with a smile to reassure her.

Seeing him look at her like that, so obviously happy to see her again, Cherish takes heart from his smile and gives his hand a squeeze. "Yes, I am back, aren't I," she chuckles nervously. "And I feel better than ever for seeing you again, Travis. How are you, how have you been without me here to look after you?"

Yes, you always did try to look after me...until this... Without realising, Travis raises his free hand to touch his ravaged cheek, a move that doesn't go unnoticed by Cherish.

Reaching up to cover his hand, she pulls it away to see for herself the damage that she had inflicted.

With a gasp of distress, Cherish can hardly breathe and Travis has to reach out to steady her.

"I did that," she gasps, her eyes wide and filling with tears. "I didn't remember, not until this moment - oh, Travis, how you must hate me?!"

Having convinced himself that he did for so many years, Travis is surprised to find that he feels only pity for the woman before him.

Taking her hand from his cheek, Travis allows his hair to cover the scars and finds it in his heart to forgive her. "It wasn't your fault, Cherish," he tells her, his voice soft and deep, soothing and kind. "You were very ill, and I'm glad to see you so much better. I doubt the passing years have been easy on you – don't punish yourself anymore."

With great difficulty, Cherish pulls herself together and wipes her face dry of any tears. But her bottom lip is still trembling and her eyes are still glistening bright as diamonds.

"I've loved you for so long, I always imagined us the way we were. I never...I didn't...oh god!"

With a trembling hand flying up to cover her mouth, Cherish moves back her chair and flees the dining room, leaving Travis shaken and staring after her.

CHAPTER TEN

"What the hell!" Catherine is on her feet, charging after the woman who has just exited the dining room in a mad dash.

Believing that she might be trying to get away, Catherine follows her but halts when she sees Cherish go into the ladies room.

Following after her, Logan arrives to find Catherine standing guard over the door to the ladies room and moves to take her arm.

"We'll be less conspicuous if we stand together over here," he tells her, drawing her reluctantly over to the reception desk. "If she tries to leave we'll be better placed to follow."

Seeing the sense in what he's saying, Catherine finally stops trying to pull out of his grasp. "If I've got bruises on my arm I'll fuck you silly when we get home!"

Laughing at her belligerent tone, Logan merely pulls her more firmly into his side. "You can do that anyway, I certainly won't protest."

But all he gets from Catherine is a deep frown. Then she smiles at a salacious and satisfying thought.

"What if I was to tie you to the bed..." she asks, her blue eyes narrowed and challenging, "...you would be all mine to do with as I will." Then her smile and her eyes take on a truly wicked look, "Scared?"

"Jesus!" Logan has to move her to cover the massive hard-on her she's just given him. "Will you behave, damn it!"

But Catherine just wiggles her bottom into his crotch enjoying this foolish interlude.

Gasping out loud, Logan quickly turns the sound into a cough at Jane's look of surprise from the other side of the reception desk. Thankfully, she had been engaged in booking someone into the hotel, otherwise she might have been shocked by their conversation.

Just then, the ladies room door opens and Cherish Wade steps out. Catherine stiffens and Logan tightens his arm about her waist to forestall any move she might make towards the other woman.

Hesitating, Cherish looks uncertain as to what she should do, but finally returns to the dining room.

"Christ, I thought she was going to make a run for it!" Catherine sags against Logan, glad of his supporting strength.

"We need to trust Travis to do his job," Logan tells her quietly, not wanting to be overheard by the attentive receptionist.

Catherine...? Catherine? Where are you? What's happening? Whats...

"Caroline!" Catherine gasps out loud.

Turning her to face him, Logan stares into her eyes but they aren't seeing him, Catherine's mind is focused elsewhere.

Caroline...can you hear me...I'm hear sis'...talk to me.

For a moment it seems the tenuous link has broken, but then Catherine hears her sister's voice in her head and almost cries with relief.

Don't know where I am...can you come get me...please...

Caroline sounds scared and very drowsy, but at least she is conscious enough to open her mind to Catherine.

Can you see anything around you, Caroline...anything that might tell us where you are?

Catherine...? Her voice is not much more than a desperate slur and it's the last Catherine can make out.

"Damn it, Caroline!" Then Catherine finds herself being held tight in Logan's arms as her tears drench his very expensive shirt.

"It's alright..." he shushes her gently, "...it's alright."

"No, it really isn't," Catherine turns her head from side to side, her forehead boring into his broad chest. "She doesn't have any idea where she is and that bitch is keeping her drugged!"

"But you made contact...right?" he asks, not having been privy to Catherine's thoughts.

"Yes – at least, Caroline made contact with me."

Moving her to sit at a table in a nook near the main entrance, Logan takes her hands reassuringly.

"If she did it once she'll do it again," he tells her, and gives Catherine's hands a gentle squeeze. "Caroline is as strong and determined as you are, my love. If there's a way out of her situation you can bet she will find it."

"I wish I could believe that," Catherine frowns over at him, her bottom lip caught between her teeth to stop it trembling.

"Believe it!" Travis orders, trying to be strong for her sake. "You need a clear mind to help Caroline; doubting her and worrying is only going to fog your thought process and put her in even more danger."

He doesn't want to hurt her, but Logan knows that the best way to rouse Catherine to action is to get her angry enough to rise to the challenge.

"You bastard! I would never put Caroline in danger!"

"Then get your act together and stop feeling sorry for yourself," Logan states bluntly. "You have a brilliant mind – start using it."

Not understanding why her husband is suddenly turning on her, Catherine feels his words deep in her still vulnerable heart.

"Get your hands off me!" Catherine pulls her hands out of his then stands tall and stiff glaring down at Logan. "I don't know where you get off talking to me like that, but I don't care! Do you hear me, Mr high and mighty Sayers, I don't bloody care!"

Without waiting for his reply, Catherine storms off going back to the lounge and orders herself a stiff drink. By the time Logan joins her, she's already downed a double whisky and is ordering another.

"Make that two," Logan tells the barman, and takes out his wallet to pay.

"I can pay for my own drinks." Catherine doesn't even look at him, simply throwing a ten pound note across the bar.

"Fine!" Logan picks up the whisky that the barman has just served him and downs it in one, then hands the man the money to pay for it.

Taking Catherine's arm, Logan forcibly marches her over to a secluded table and pushes her down into a chair. "Don't even think about it," he tells her when Catherine puts her hands on the arms of the chair in order to push up from it. "Focus all that anger on finding Caroline and you might just succeed!"

"You bastard!"

"So you said," Logan sighs, steeling himself so as not to soften. "Now, how about we consider what we're going to do when Travis and Cherish come out of the dining room?"

"Don't call her that!" Catherine glares over at him as Logan takes a seat.

"Fine..." Logan concedes easily, "...we'll call her Ms Wade-"

"Just Wade will do! She doesn't deserve your pleasantries."

"We can hardly address her that way in front of Travis," he tells her with a raised brow. "If he invites her up to the penthouse-"

"WHAT, are you crazy?!" Catherine sits upright, her spine rigid. "You think Travis is cold enough to entertain his wife's captor in her own home?"

"I think Travis will be willing to do anything to put Ms Wade at her ease in order to extract information from her, yes," Logan confirms calmly.

"So that's what you would do if this were me being held God knows where?"

Feeling decidedly uncomfortable at that thought, Logan sidesteps a direct answer. "I would do anything it took if someone were stupid enough to take you from me."

His voice had stayed low and almost calm, but Catherine had heard the threat...no, the promise of physical harm to any such person. And for some reason, it calms her.

With a frown and a question in her eyes, Catherine reaches across the table to take his hand. "You really love me, don't you?"

"How many times do I have to tell you, woman – yes, damn it, I love you more than my own life. Now, I need another drink." And turning in his chair, Logan signals to a waiter, but before he can place his order Logan spots Travis and Wade coming out of the dining room.

"Sorry, we won't be staying after all," Logan smiles briefly at the waiter who gives a polite nod and walks away. Then, turning to Catherine, he says, "They're out. Just casually look over my shoulder and see what they're doing."

Leaning across the table, Catherine can indeed see Travis and Wade standing near the lounge doors ready to leave. "They appear to be in deep discussion about something," she tells Logan. "Yes, he's offering her a lift home but Wade doesn't seem keen to take him up on it." Watching the interaction between her brother-in-law and Wade, Catherine silently seethes at the intimate way Wade keeps touching his arm, sliding her hand up and down it as a lover might do.

"What else is going on?" Logan asks, watching his wife's face contort with unspoken emotions.

"What...oh...she's getting cosy with him, touching him like they're a couple, or some such shit!"

"He's just playing along with her," Logan assures Catherine. "Travis is probably cringing inside, but he'll play up to her if he thinks it will lead to getting Caroline back home safely."

"I suppose. Hey, they're leaving!" Catherine exclaims suddenly. "What do we do now?"

"You stay here..." he tells her, and sees the instant panic in her eyes, "...you stay here and I'll follow them. You can't be seen – you forget how much you and Caroline are alike, it would cause a major distraction if she were to see you."

Reluctantly, Catherine nods and Logan is gone before she can change her mind. But it's absolute torture not to know what is going on.

If he's taken her up to the penthouse, to Caroline's home and where their daughters are sleeping... Bloody hell, I want to commit murder so bad I can almost feel my hands around her flaming neck!

Caroline? Caroline...can you hear me?

It had only been a shot in the dark, a need to reach out to her sister, and Catherine is shocked when her sister's voice comes into her head.

Catherine...are you there...?

Yes, it's me...you can hear me. Catherine thinks stupidly.

Yes...I think the drugs are wearing off...but it's hard to think...hard to make sense of anything...

That's alright, just keep trying, Catherine urges her. *Wade is here, at the hotel.* But Catherine refrains from saying 'with Travis'. *We're going to follow her home – see where she lives – that could be where she's holding you.*

Catherine... Catherine begins to panic, her sister's voice is becoming drowsy and faint again.

Caroline – don't give in to the drugs – you've got to fight them – do you hear me, fight them Caroline!

But her sister's voice doesn't answer and Catherine knows that their connection has been lost.

"What is it?" Logan asks when he retakes his seat, having moved the chair to sit beside her. "You look pale and sad, what's happened?" And he looks around to find the cause of her apparent distress.

"Caroline," she states simply, then turns her head into his chest and begins to cry unashamedly.

"It's alright, we'll find her," Logan assures her as he pulls her more firmly into his side and strokes her hair. "Travis got one of the hotel's courtesy cars to take Wade home – he went with her so he'll be able to tell us where she lives."

Taking the handkerchief Logan is holding out to her, Catherine dries her eyes and tidies herself up. "I never used to cry," she sniffs, angry with herself. "Now I seem to cry at the drop of a hat – that's your fault!" And she gives Logan a poke in the ribs. "You've made me all mushy and soft headed – I liked it better when I was in control, when feelings didn't get inside of me."

Chuckling softly, Logan hugs her to him again.

"Well I like the new you just fine. You can cry all over me any time the mood takes you," and he kisses the top of her head as Catherine leans into him again.

By the time Travis returns, Catherine and Logan are seated in the hotel lobby waiting for him.

Crossing to them, Travis has to force himself to look at Catherine – it hurts that she looks so identical to his missing wife.

"Shall we go up..." he invites cordially, "...we have a lot to discuss."

CHAPTER ELEVEN

On entering the penthouse, Travis crosses the lounge to pour himself a brandy and offers his guests a drink also.

"No, that's alright, I've already had more than I should considering I've got to drive home," Logan admits. "But you have one, if you like," he offers Catherine.

"Don't let that stop you..." Travis looks over at Logan, his face tired and his brown eyes clearly showing the strain he's under, "...the courtesy car can take you home. I'll get someone to follow in your car."

"In that case, I'll have a brandy, too," Logan nods, having smelt the fine spirit that Travis is drinking.

"Catherine...?" Travis holds up a bottle of white wine and pours a glass when she nods her acceptance.

Joining them in the lounge area, Travis takes a seat opposite Catherine and Logan, silently contemplating his drink.

"I don't know how I did it," he says to no one in particular. "I was sat right there, outside the house where my wife is probably being held captive, and I didn't go in."

He looks gaunt, haunted, and thoroughly disgusted with himself, but Travis is wise enough to know that he couldn't have done anything differently.

"I think we'd better call Frank," Catherine suggests. "He'll be grateful that you had the strength to drive away, believe me," she consoles her brother-in-law. "Caroline might well be in that house, but what if she isn't? What if Wade is hiding her somewhere — you barging in there would have alerted her to the fact that we know she's the one holding Caroline. She could do a runner if she even suspects that we're on to her, then we might never bring my sister home."

If possible, Travis pales further, but he nods in agreement. "Call your Inspector friend; we'll do whatever he suggests."

Getting to her feet, Catherine takes out her mobile and calls Inspector Frank Harper.

"Hi, sorry to call so late..." she apologises, suddenly realising the time, "...but we know where Wade lives now.

Travis took her home from the hotel not more than an hour ago."

Listening to Frank ask for the address and tell her that he'll get a man over there right away, Catherine feels a small knot of hope begin to stir.

"Ok, at least that's something," she agrees when Frank tells her that they will be keeping Wade under 24 hour observation. "You'll let us know if anything develops?"

Having been assured that he will indeed let them know of any developments, Catherine puts the mobile back in her pocket and retakes her seat to fill Logan and Travis in on the conversation. "So she won't be able to go anywhere without the police knowing about it," she finishes.

"Then there's nothing else to do tonight," Logan states and gets to his feet. "If you don't need us to stay, we'll take you up on that car and get off home."

During the ride home, Logan and Catherine sit together in the back seat of the courtesy car and try to relax. But Catherine's mind just can't let go.

"Do you think we're making progress?" she asks Logan, but doesn't give him time to answer. "I think we're making progress – at least, we now know where Wade is living, you have her details and should be able to tell us where she moves to, if she does. But is she holding Caroline at the house she's renting now?"

Frowning, taking only a second's breath, Catherine continues, "I'm not sure that really makes sense. If Wade knows she's looking to move – rent or buy – it wouldn't be wise to keep Caroline at this house. She'd have to risk moving her to the new house without being seen – that's very risky, right?"

When Logan doesn't immediately reply, Catherine turns her face up to frown at him. "What...you don't agree? Say something!"

Smiling, Logan puts an arm about her shoulders and gives her a patient hug. "I was just waiting for you to give me the chance," he chuckles, and puts a knuckle under her chin to lift her lips high enough to kiss. "I do agree. We have to factor in the possibility that Ms Wade is not thinking as clearly as you are. She's a diagnosed schizophrenic – that raises all kinds of possible scenarios. What if she's taking her meds and is thinking rationally – could she be clever enough to conceal Caroline somewhere we haven't even thought of...yet," he adds when Catherine's eyes cloud over with worry. "Then again, she might think she's taking her meds correctly but due to the stresses and distractions of the kidnap and concealment of Caroline, Ms Wade could be skipping a few doses and might then become unstable."

"Or she could be off them entirely and be completely off her rocker!" Catherine closes her eyes on the thought of her sister in the hands of a deranged kidnapper.

"Yes, that is a possibility, I won't deny that," Logan admits reluctantly. "But she was holding herself together enough to have dinner in a public place without exhibiting any psychotic traits."

"She ran off to the loo," Catherine reminds him.

"Yes, but even that was understandable," Logan reasons quietly. "She's been locked away for the last 18 years and, from what you read in her medical notes, she was in a catatonic state for most of that. Seeing Travis again must have been stressful and full of emotions that she isn't used to dealing with. I think running to the ladies room was pretty tame under the circumstances."

"Are you sticking up for her?!" Catherine has moved forward in her seat to look Logan right in the eyes, and hers are giving off sparks.

"Not exactly..." he begins gently, "...but you can't demonise the woman either. She's ill – when she's on her meds she's probably one of the nicest women you're ever likely to meet."

The sparks in Catherine's eyes just ignited into the fiery pits of hell, and they are all but consuming Logan where he sits. "Ok, maybe not that nice – but she's a human being, not some demon from hell."

"And I should feel sorry for her?!" Catherine is not amused, her sense of outrage on Caroline's behalf clouding her judgement. "So if she just happens to slit my sister's throat in a psychotic frenzy I should just forgive and forget, is that it?! Well I won't – and if you can't get behind me on this I'd rather you stay right out of my way. I'm going to bring my sister home alive no matter what it takes or who I have to hurt to do it!"

You protect your own! Our boys don't yet know how lucky they are to have a mother like you – and you have no idea how wonderful you really are. I'm not just behind you on this, I'm right alongside of you. And if it comes to dealing with Ms Wade face to face, I'll be right in front of you!

"You don't need to doubt my commitment to bringing Caroline home safe," Logan tells her, his hand moving to gently cup her cheek. "I'll do whatever it takes to make that happen."

Hesitating, Catherine looks deep into Logan's eyes as if reading his soul. Then she sags forward, all the fight going out of her, and lays her cheek against the wall of muscle that is his chest and listens to the solid, reassuring beat of his large heart.

"I love you, Logan... I really mean that."

"I love you, too. My very own firebrand," he chuckles softly. "I'd definitely want you on my side if ever I were in trouble."

"Really...?"

"Absolutely!"

Sleep does not come easily that night – both are troubled by 'what ifs' and the various scenarios running around in their heads. When morning finally arrives, Catherine and Logan do not wake feeling rested and refreshed.

Adam had woken for a feed in the night so, of course, he'd woken up his brother, Andrew.

At least they sleep later in the morning when they've had a night feed – I need a long hot shower to wake me up.

Rolling reluctantly out of bed, Catherine pads off to the bathroom and shouts, "Going shower – I'll be a while," over her shoulder.

Sure enough, after a minute or two standing stock still under the soothing hot water raining down on her head, Catherine's mind and body begin to emerge from the fuddled fog of too little sleep.

A groan of pure bliss rolls out of her throat and causes Logan to smile as he joins her in the bathroom. Watching her soap her body, cupping her full round breast and moving a deft hand down to the v between her legs, Logan decides he wants to hear her groan some more, and just for him.

"Here, let me help you with that," and cupping the liquid soap in his hands he rubs them together under the hot water then spreads the lather over her breasts.

She doesn't protest. Catherine has been so pent up with worry and emotions that Logan's ministrations are welcomed.

Allowing her head to rest back against the tiled wall, Catherine wallows in the feel of his searching hands. Slowly, and with such carnal expertise as only intimate lovers have, Logan explores all of her hidden places.

Her moans are music to his ears, and he wants to hear more. Pushing her legs wider apart, Logan moves between her thighs and takes her into his mouth.

Moans turn into little screams of pleasure, and then pleading for more...more...more... And Logan gives her more, increasing his need of her until it becomes almost painful.

He is hard as iron by the time he stands up in front of Catherine and doesn't hesitate to plunge into the heat of her.

He isn't gentle, that isn't what either of them needs and he knows it. Catherine's legs wrap themselves around his waist and she is using them to pull him into her, harder, faster, she just can't get enough of him.

The heat of the water flowing over them, the feel of flesh pounding into flesh, the release of pent up energy flowing freely between them, all add up to a climax that is soul shattering.

Their bodies throb and pulsate, their hearts hammer in their chests, and their lungs drag in much needed air – yet still they are joined, and Logan doesn't appear to be completely sated.

Slowly he begins to move inside her again, and Catherine simply has to hold on. His deep voice whispers crudely in her ear, telling her what he wants and what he expects. He's giving her no choice, his hands are moving over her body again then move behind her to cup her bottom and knead her buttocks until, very gently, his little finger pushes its way into her anus.

Stiffening at first, Catherine gasps with shock but Logan doesn't withdraw his finger, just allows her to get used to the new sensation.

Continuing to move slowly in and out, his manhood still filling her gloriously, Logan begins to knead her buttocks again and increases the pressure from his little finger.

"Logan...I don't think..." But then she can't think, doesn't want to think, he's driving her body up to heights of pleasure it has never experienced before.

"Oh god, Logan!"

Her climax is even more soul shattering than before, it never seems to end but rolls throughout her body causing every nerve and synapse to fire off incredible sparks of pleasure. And Logan is looking very pleased with himself.

"You're going to kill me!" she mumbles into his shoulder, too shattered to lift her head.

His deep, rumbling laughter judders his body enough to make Catherine writhe against him. Logan is still inside her, and even while he's losing his erection she can still feel the length of him moving against her sensitised flesh.

"Let me down," she tells him, pushing against Logan's chest to free herself, and reluctantly he lowers Catherine's feet to the floor.

But before she can move away from him, Logan takes her face between his two large hands and begins to kiss her soundly.

Water is rivuletting down their cheeks unnoticed as Logan shows her the depth of his love. Then, lifting his head, he looks into her dazed eyes and says, "I'm behind everything you do, wholeheartedly and without reservations – you'll do me the honour of not doubting that in future."

With a silent nod, Catherine moves forward to seal her promise with a kiss. "I love you, Logan...I have no doubts about that. But I need to work on my trust issues; and they are my issues, I want you to know that I know that."

"Good enough. Now, let's get working on getting Caroline home again."

CHAPTER TWELVE

Sharing a corner of Catherine's desk, Logan works alongside her and Emma in order to track down an arsonist and a kidnapper.

Logan has finished accumulating information on a number of suspected cases of arson, but none of them relate to a time when Cherish could possibly have been responsible.

Having moved on, he is now following up on the information that Catherine gained from the Fire Chief's reports – traces of petrol and remnants of a particular type of rope were found at both crime scenes. If he can find records of recent sales of both items, Logan might be able to trace them back to the buyer.

Having heard a knock on the office door, three heads lift and turn to look at it in unison.

"Come in," Logan invites, his brows pulled into a frown. His father would just come in, he knows, but Linda would knock and wait but never normally bothers the girls when they were working. *Not unless it's some kind of emergency? Not another fire, surely!*

"I'm so sorry to disturb you all, but Inspector Harper and Detective Shivers say they need a word," Linda tells them, and stands to one side to let the two men enter the office.

"You all look very industrious, I must say," Frank Harper smiles. "Since we saw you yesterday, a member of the public handed in a small number of items that we'd like you to take a look at," and Frank looks directly at Catherine then takes out a clear plastic property bag from his overcoat pocket.

Holding the bag out to her, Frank watches as Catherine walks hesitantly across the room towards him. Not taking the items out, he allows Catherine to finger the bag in order to move the items within for a better look.

"These are Caroline's," she states positively, though she has no idea how she got the words out. Her mouth has gone dry and her usually sharp mind feels dull and fearful. "At least...the earrings and bracelet are – I'm not sure about the ring. Where were they found? Have you shown them to Travis?"

Nodding, the inspector says, "We have, and Mr Lovett identified the ring as one he recently gifted to his wife."

Logan is watching his wife; concerned by her sudden pallor he moves quickly to pull a chair up behind her. "Just sit down for a minute," he urges, and gives Catherine a feather-light push on the shoulder that is all it takes to buckle her knees.

At just that precise moment, the office door opens again only this time it is Adrianne who walks through it.

Feeling totally confused, and not a little faint, Catherine frowns up and asks, "What the hell are you doing here?"

Getting the feeling that she's walked in on something important, Adrianne doesn't take offence at her sister's lack of greeting.

"I was going stir-crazy at home so I got Robert to bring down," Adrianne tells Catherine, and looks around the room at everyone who is now staring back at her. "Sorry, did I come in at a bad time?"

Sloane Shivers has taken a marked step back, as if she is some kind of explosive device that might go off at any time.

Having come to join the rest of the group, Emma moves to his side and whispers, "Coward — and you reckon you want a couple of your own?!"

Giving her a sidelong glare, Sloane ignores her taunt and stays right where he is.

"Ah, Mrs Kingsley, may I get you a chair?" Frank offers politely, not quite as worried by the imminent arrival of a baby, but not taking any unnecessary chances either.

Accepting his offer, Adrianne sits next to Catherine and holds her sister's hand. "What's going on, you look awful?"

Rubbing the back of the hand still holding the property bag over her tired eyes, Catherine shakes her head in a defeated gesture then takes the bull by the horns and confesses all. "We didn't want to worry you..." she begins tentatively, giving Adrianne's hand a reassuring squeeze, "...but Caroline has gone missing. We think she was taken by someone she gave a lift to the morning after the cinema fire."

For just a second all breathing in the room stops and time seems to stand still. But far from becoming hysterical – or going into labour as everyone fears she might – Adrianne stiffens her spine and looks around the small crowd of people then back to her sister.

"And just when were you planning to tell me this?" she asks, knowing full well that Catherine hadn't planned to tell her anything at all. When Catherine doesn't answer, Adrianne continues, her voice now cold and accusatory, "I suppose dad knows – I saw him after you visited him yesterday afternoon – he didn't say anything to me either!"

"Well lucky you..." Catherine snaps back, coming out of her stupor, "...because he had plenty to say to me, I can tell you!"

"Good! I hope he tore a strip off you – you deserved it!" Then Adrianne gets to her feet and walks right up to Frank Harper. "And you should have informed me of my sister's abduction..." she tells him, poking a sharp finger into his chest, "...what kind of a police station are you running anyway?!"

Sloane takes a step forward to stand by his boss, but very quickly regrets the move when Adrianne rounds on him. "And you're just as bad! Standing there quivering at the sight of a pregnant woman – we are not delicate flowers that will wither with the telling of bad news – you should have told me!"

Taking his life in his hands, Logan reaches out to touch Adrianne's shoulders and when she whirls on him he readies himself for her attack, but forestalls it by pulling her into a brotherly hug.

At first she beats her fists on his arms, but Logan continues to hold her until Adrianne stills. "We were wrong..." he admits softly, holding her away from him to look down into her beautiful Irish blue eyes "...but we did what we did because we care about you. No one here wants to be the cause of any harm coming to you or that precious baby you're carrying."

Guiding her back to the seat next to Catherine, Logan gives her a warm smile then moves away to let the sisters talk.

"You should have told me," Adrianne says more quietly.

This time it is Catherine who reaches out to take Adrianne's hand before admitting, "Yes, you're right. But so is Logan – we were only trying to protect you; had we thought there was anything you could do to help we would have come to you sooner."

"What is that?" Adrianne points to the property bag that Catherine is still holding.

Bloody hell, now what?! Knowing that she can't lie, not after Adrianne has made it clear that she wants to know what's going on, Catherine takes a deep breath and lets it out slowly.

"Frank brought these round to get a second opinion on their owner's identity," Catherine sighs, and drops the bag into Adrianne's free hand.

As she fingers the bag in the same way that Catherine had, the stud post of one of the earrings pokes through and makes contact with her skin.

The moment she felt the gold metal against her skin, Adrianne began seeing images of Caroline in her head. There was nothing subtle about them, they were crystal clear and if they would just stay still long enough Adrianne felt she might be able to reach out and touch her sister.

Hearing someone gasping for breath, Adrianne eventually realises that it is her.

"Call an ambulance," she can hear Catherine shout. "Maybe you should lie her down on the floor," she hears Emma suggest, the voices sounding as if from a distance.

"No, no, I'm alright..." Adrianne moans, finally coming to herself, "...but I could use a glass of water."

Sloane takes a clean mug over to the cold water fountain and fills it half full, then offers it to Adrianne.

After gulping it down, she sits back in her chair and tries to calm her breathing while everyone else looks on warily.

"I'm not in labour..." she announces finally, "...but other than that, I have no idea what just happened!"

"What do you mean, you have no idea," Catherine demands, fear for her baby sister making her snap unreasonably. "You looked like you were in the grip of...of...something," Catherine splutters, not knowing how best to describe her sister's behaviour.

"And...I was...I just don't know what," Adrianne frowns, trying to make sense of what just happened. "One minute I was just looking at Caroline's jewellery, the next... Well, this is going to sound really weird..." and she looks at the faces surrounding her, "...but...the next thing I know she was in my head. Just...sort of flashing images, but so clear I felt I could touch her – only they didn't stay still long enough for me to try."

Then Adrianne laughs, not hysterically but verging on it. "And I sound like a loon!"

"No, m'dear, you really don't," Frank Harper tells her before his eyes turn to Catherine. "Perhaps it would be as well to get Farraday here asap, don't you think?"

"Farraday – who's Farraday?" Adrianne asks.

"He might come quicker if you gave him a call," Catherine nods at Frank in agreement.

Deciding that she's had enough of being talked over, Adrianne stands up with a ramrod straight spine – which thrusts her protruding belly out alarmingly – and calls a halt. "Enough, already!"

Her usually soft spoken voice brings everyone to a halt instantly – or it could have been the sight of her extremely pregnant abdomen and her hands clasped ominously on either side of it, Adrianne would consider that later.

"You're all either trying to send me to the hospital or calling some man I don't believe I've ever heard of," Adrianne pants out. "How about someone explains what the heck is going on and let me make my own decisions – how about that!"

Emma looks incredulous; she's never seen 'the quiet one' go off like that before. And turning to Catherine she whispers, "She's your sister alright, now deal!"

But rather than 'deal' with her sister in front of an audience, Catherine gets to her feet and grabs Adrianne's hand, then drags her out and along the corridor to their private sitting room.

"Ok, sit!" she tells Adrianne ungraciously, yet her sister complies without complaint. But Catherine begins to pace the carpet, more able to think on her feet. "You know that Caroline and I have a link – some kind of communication which has been getting stronger the more we're in each other's company – right?"

And, watching for Adrianne's nod of agreement, Catherine goes on to explain further. "Well, I seem to remember telling you about my other experiences – the ones where I see things in my head, nothing to do with Caroline."

"Yes, though I was never clear exactly what you meant. I just thought it was like a...well...a very well developed instinct. You're very clever, you know," Adrianne adds as if that explains everything.

Breathing out a long sigh, Catherine feels her heart sink. *Now my baby sister is going to think I'm a loony-toon!* "No, sweetie, that's not quite it. I've been getting what some people would call 'visions'," she grimaces, hating the sound of that word and the look of horror on her sister's face. "I thought you understood – that's why I've been seeing Farraday – he's helping me to get to grips with it."

Then she surprises Adrianne by laughing, "He's got an even worse deal than I do – he actually walks in his visions." But her laughter quickly dies as the look of horror on Adrianne's face increases.

Moving to sit next to her sister, Catherine pats her hand, saying, "Sorry, sorry, you didn't really need to know that. But what you do need to know is that Farraday...Neil, is brilliant at what he does. He can help us to find out what happened just now."

Then Catherine considers how much more to tell Adrianne, fearing that she may have frightened her too much already. "I'm not sure why, but I think I saw some of what you did – the images of Caroline," she clarifies, her voice tailing off to whisper.

"You were in my head?!" Adrianne gasps, shocked by the thought.

Thinking that her sister was now regarding her as a freak, Catherine jumps to her feet and flies into a temper – a reaction born of years of protecting herself from just such taunts that had been thrown at her for most of her young life.

"I didn't ask to be," she flares, her arms flailing in the air. "I didn't ask for any of this...this freaky brain...this freaky 'gift'," and she mimes quotation marks in the air. But before she can draw another angry breath to continue her tirade, Logan steps into the room.

"I thought we'd agreed that word is never to be used in this house, or in any way in connection to you, ever again?" His deep voice is steady but brooks no argument, and his eyes tell her not to bother trying. "Now, if you ladies have finished your confab, perhaps we may return to the office and get this matter sorted out." And without waiting to see if they would follow, Logan gives them a polite nod, does a stiff about turn and strides off.

Adrianne looks stricken, but Catherine actually laughs, though nervously. "That's his Etonian voice..." Catherine whispers as they do indeed follow Logan out, "...he uses it when he's feeling a bit peeved – or when he's trying to win a point and tries to sway the argument by sounding brainy. Which he is," Catherine concedes," and is surprised to hear her sister chuckling.

"He sounds perfect for you," Adrianne whispers back, just before they re enter the office.

"Ah, just so," Inspector Harper smiles and greets them inanely. And, after watching the two women retake their seats, he looks from one to the other with a quizzically raised brow.

But Catherine still doesn't know how Adrianne feels about working with Farraday. "Adrianne...?"

Hesitating only briefly, Adrianne nods her agreement then says, "But I'm not going to do anything that puts my son at risk!" And her arms wrap around her stomach protectively.

CHAPTER THIRTEEN

It doesn't take long for Neil Farraday to work out what it was that Adrianne had experienced. But now he wants to repeat the process, to monitor her reactions and document it.

"It seems evident that you need physical contact with the object to make the connection," he observes while watching Adrianne finger the transparent property bag. "Perhaps you could manipulate the earring stud to protrude a little, as it did before?"

Doing as he asked, Adrianne wiggles the stem of the earring through the tiny hole it had made previously. The she looks up at Neil, "Now what?"

"Just touch it and see," he advises.

But when Adrianne's finger presses gently on the metal stem, not a single image enters her mind and she looks about her feeling extremely foolish.

Shrugging her shoulders she looks up at Neil and again asks, "Now what?"

"You didn't get anything?" he asks disappointed.

"Not a flicker," Adrianne confirms.

"Hmm, that's rather unusual after such a strong reaction the first time," Neil observes frowning. "Are you doing it in exactly the same way as you did before?"

Then Adrianne becomes annoyed, her embarrassment making her unusually snappy, "I didn't 'do' anything before – I simply held the bag, felt the post of the earring press into my finger and the images just came flooding into my head!"

Reaching across, Catherine places a comforting hand over her sister's, but then the world turns on its head again.

Neil goes into an ecstatic dance of hoping, clapping his hands and grinning manically. This is exactly what he'd been hoping for!

Looking at Catherine with wide, frightened eyes, Adrianne pulls her hand away. "It isn't me, it's you!" she accuses, then realises what she's just said. "No, I didn't mean it like that...I just meant..."

But Catherine has risen from her chair and backed away. "That's ok, I know exactly what you meant." And she runs from the room, locking herself in the bedroom.

Less than half an hour later, Logan knocks on the door and asks to be let in.

Hesitating momentarily, Catherine eventually does so. "I suppose you think I made a right fool of myself?" she mumbles pitifully, turning her back to walk away.

"I don't think any such thing," Logan tells her, his large hands on her shoulders to halt her retreat. "Adrianne has gone home, though she wanted to stay and sort things out between you – I told her it would be better to let you calm down first."

Turning then, Catherine buries her face in Logan's chest and holds him tight around the waist. "Thank you. I'm no good at all that sister stuff – I'd only have upset her anyway. It's what I'm good at."

"Will you stop!" Logan tightens his arms about her, but he's far from happy to hear Catherine knocking herself again. "First you use the banned 'F' word and now you're claiming to be a total failure in the sister department – none of which is true!"

"It's alright – I know who and what I am, I learned to accept myself years ago."

"Oh really...is that right!" Logan takes her by the shoulders and gives Catherine a gentle shake, though it still causes her head to bobble backwards and forwards uncomfortably. "You may hate to admit your feelings; you're so frightened of getting knocked back that you'd rather cut your right hand off than let anyone see how much you really care – but that doesn't mean those feelings don't exist, or hurt. It's part of the process, Catherine. If you don't open yourself up to the possibility of being hurt you also shut yourself off from ever being loved!"

"But...I have you..." she tells him, looking up at Logan with uncertain eyes, "...that must mean that I opened myself up to loving you, and you could destroy me so very easily."

Hugging her to him again, Logan tries to swallow the lump in his throat. "I'm just the first step, Catherine – though it was a fairly easy one to take given the fact that I'm crazy about you. But, I'm very glad you did," he chuckles and places a kiss on the top of her head.

"You're right...I know you're right...but I'm also scared. Just look at me and Caroline – we couldn't be closer if we tried. And I love her so much, the thought that she might come to harm frightens me half to death; I don't want to feel that kind of fear again, that depth of loss," Catherine admits, remembering how debilitating it had been after losing her mother.

"So you're going to take a step back from Adrianne too?

"I..no...I don't know," Catherine tries to think more rationally.

Her emotions have always seemed to cloud Catherine's judgement, which is one reason she's tried so hard to suppress them.

"No, I don't want to step away from Adrianne," she finally admits with a sigh. "She's my baby sister, I want to be there for her, and her baby, to help in any way I can but-"

"No buts! Just take it one step at a time, and once Caroline is back home again you'll feel a lot more settled," Logan assures her.

I know what this is all about; you are so frightened of losing Caroline that you're already shielding yourself against the pain. And I can't blame you – what happened when you were a child would be enough to crush anyone; the real miracle is that you came through it as whole as you did!

"You really believe we'll get her back...?"

"I have no doubts...do you?"

Leaning away from Logan, Catherine suddenly smiles and shakes her head. "No...because we're not going to let anything happen to her. Come on, let's get back to work!"

A couple of hours later, tired but encouraged by their findings, Catherine and Logan join Henry and Linda for dinner in the kitchen.

"How's it going?" Henry asks, his expression one of deep concern.

"Actually, we caught a break this afternoon," Logan announces. "I managed to track down a large purchase of the exact same rope as was used to tie off the exits at both the school and the cinema."

Smiling proudly up at him, Catherine adds, "We're going to visit the shop tomorrow morning — they've agreed to let us view their in-store security footage."

"Good. Good. That sounds very positive," Henry smiles and nods happily.

"You realise that Ms Wade may not be on it," Linda cautions gently. "I mean, it's very possible that she paid someone to purchase it for her. She's been very clever so far, why take the risk - most shops do have security cameras now."

Frowning, Catherine considers this but decides not to let it dampen her mood. "You're right, of course, but she's bound to slip up some time. We just have to make sure that we're around when she does – only by checking out every lead will we stand a chance of doing that."

"Absolutely!" Logan agrees, glad that Catherine is able to stay optimistic.

But the day isn't over for any of them, and Cherish Wade has plans to spend her evening with Travis.

Dressing carefully in a simple blue calf-length dress and matching cardigan, Cherish heads for The Lovett Hotel. She doesn't want to appear too glamorous, but simply smart and attractive.

"The last thing I want is Travis thinking that I'm some sort of femme fatal," she tells her reflection as she turns to admire her trim figure in a shop window. "I want him to remember how much he loves me...just as I love him. And he will," she smiles happily, her certainty giving her the courage to go on.

"Would you mind telling Travis Lovett that Cherish Wade is here to see him?" she asks the hotel's receptionist.

"Of course, miss. Would you mind taking a seat for a moment," and the receptionist holds out a hand to indicate the nearby comfy seating.

As soon as the woman is out of ear-shot, the receptionist does as she's been asked and relates the message to her boss, Travis Lovett.

"Alright, Shirley – offer Ms Wade some refreshment and inform her that I will be down momentarily," Travis instructs, somewhat taken aback by Cherish Wade's unexpected arrival.

Adrianne had insisted that Ellisa, Caroline's PA, return to the hotel to help out with the girls, once she became aware of Caroline's abduction. And truth be told, Travis has been glad of the help.

"I'm needed downstairs," he tells Ellisa after checking that his daughters are settled for the night. "I'm hoping I won't be gone long, but if you need me just call down to reception."

"Don't worry..." Ellisa smiles reassuringly, "...the girls have gone down good as gold, and I'm fine."

By the time Travis gets down to the lobby, Cherish is drinking the tea that Shirley provided.

"Cherish..." Travis addresses her cordially, "...this is something of a surprise – is there a problem?"

"Please, come and take tea with me..." she invites, patting a nearby seat, "...I asked your kind receptionist for a second cup."

Taking the seat, Travis allows Cherish to pour him a cup of tea and notes that she still remembers how he takes it.

"I came to apologise," Cherish tells him while handing him his tea. "My behaviour last evening was over emotional and deplorable. It wasn't my intention to embarrass you, Travis."

"I wasn't embarrassed, but I was concerned for your well-being," Travis clarifies. "That is why I insisted on taking you home."

Reaching out to cover his hand with one of her own, Cherish looks adoringly into his eyes. "You always have been a caring soul; it's what I've always loved about you."

Looking at Cherish, searching her lovely face for signs of duplicity or cunning, Travis is all the more disturbed to fine none.

If she were feigning her feelings, trying to trap him in some way, Travis would feel more able to deal with Cherish. But what can he do with a woman who has emerged as if from a long sleep, still in love with her fiancée.

Taking the hand laid over his, Travis tries to explain the situation to her as gently as he can.

"Cherish, when we were together I loved you so completely, but that was 18 years ago and life has had to move on," he tells her softly. "I am married now, and father to two adorable little girls, but you will always hold a very special place in my heart."

"And you will ever stay in mine," she smiles, gripping his fingers with hers. "Do you remember when we decided to get engaged?" she asks, chuckling delicately. "My mother was askance and your parents were outraged – my father was the only one to give us his blessing." Looking at their joined hands, Cherish's eyes go distant with remembering, "I miss my father; he always understood me best."

Unsure of what to say for the best, Travis watches Cherish struggle with her loss. It is plainly difficult for her, having only learned of her parent's demise during the process of her discharge from the psychiatric unit she was living in.

"What can I do to help you, Cherish? You've obviously made great strides in coping with your illness – I want to help ensure that you stay well, that you go on to live a happy and fulfilled life," Travis declares, and finds that he means every word.

"Yes, I believe you do," Cherish smiles tremulously. "And I will; with your help I will be happy and I will be fulfilled – I just need some time, and I need to see you, Travis. I don't have anyone else," she adds, disarmingly sincere.

"Unfortunately, time is something that I have very little of to spare at the moment," Travis sighs heavily. "I don't know if you've heard, but my wife, Caroline, has gone missing. I believe she gave you a lift home the morning after the cinema fire – unfortunately she never made it back again."

"She... Oh no, that can't be," Cherish exclaims, her eyes going round with apparent shock. "That woman was your wife?!"

"Yes, so you see...my time is taken up with searching for her. But once I've got her back..." Travis leaves that thought hanging in the air then lifts his hands, letting them fall helplessly into his lap. "I just can't think of anything else right now – I'm sure you understand."

"Yes...yes of course. Oh you poor man, you must be distraught!"

"I would be, if it weren't for my daughters – I have to hold myself together for them; they already sense that something is wrong," Travis explains. Then he stands, gives Cherish a polite bow and excuses himself. "I'm sure I will see you again, Cherish, but for now I must get back to my daughters."

You see, I told you he wouldn't have time for you while 'she' still lives. Now maybe you'll listen to me and finish her!

"Shut up!" Cherish growls at the voice in her head. "Not yet; just give me some time to plan things out. But soon, I promise."

The people here don't want you – just remember the way they washed their hands of you. It's time to pay them back...make them wish they'd never had you locked away. Away from Travis...

CHAPTER FOURTEEN

When Catherine and Logan enter the hardware shop in Bolderton, it is with hope and trepidation pounding equally in their hearts.

"Hopefully they'll have taken a note of the transaction date and time on their system," Catherine whispers to Logan. "It'll save us a lot of time trawling through the security footage if they have.

Going to the small checkout desk, Logan asks to speak to the manager, gives their names and tells the young woman that they are expected.

Pressing a bell under the counter, the girl tells a young man to fetch Mr Alexander and gives them the visitors' names.

A small man, as round as he is tall, comes towards them from the rear of the shop, a smile causing his piggy eyes to appear closed.

Holding out his pudgy hand, Mr Alexander introduces himself and says, "Please, come through to the back, I've already lined up the transaction you were interested in viewing."

Catherine raises an approving brow a Logan as they both follow the man out.

"I have seen many programmes on the television where the security camera footage was almost useless," Mr Alexander tells them with a disdainful shake of his head. "For this reason I made sure that my camera system was of excellent quality – what is the use of capturing a thief on camera if he cannot be identified from the footage?" he asks, plainly not understanding the logic of some people.

"I quite agree," Catherine tells him seriously, and just hopes that Mr Alexander's security video lives up to the hype.

It does. Not only have they got the transaction on tape, they have a crystal clear picture of the man's face as he obligingly looks into the camera's lens.

"You were right, Mr Alexander..." Catherine smiles and nods at the man appreciatively, "...this is excellent quality. Is it digital?"

Returning her smile with a proud flush to his cheeks, Mr Alexander offers to burn a cd copy of the relevant footage. "It is a simple matter..." he continues happily, "...no trouble at all."

But before he can insert a disc, Catherine asks him to rewind the footage. "I'd like to see if the woman we're looking for is anywhere in the background. She may have picked out what she wanted then got the man to pay for it," she explains.

"Ah, yes, very good," Mr Alexander holds a finger in the air to signal that it will take only a moment.

Rewinding to the moment the man walks into the shop, it is clear that he enters alone. But after a moment's disappointment, Catherine asks him to wind it back again, just a little further.

This time Catherine isn't looking at the man as he enters the shop, she is looking at which direction he came from and any vehicles present.

"There, look..." Catherine points to a black taxi, "...Wade could be waiting for him inside. Could you wind forward again, Mr Alexander, I just want to see if he gets in the taxi after he leaves the shop."

It is a limited view of the outside, but when the man leaves he definitely gets in the taxi.

"Brilliant! Now we have a chance to trace it back to whoever booked it," Catherine exclaims, and gives Logan and Mr Alexander one of her brightest smiles.

"So, my good camera worked for you," Mr Alexander declares proudly.

"It certainly did! Congratulations, Mr Alexander, you may have just given us the clue that breaks the arsonist cases," Catherine tells him, her blue eyes gleaming with possibilities.

"The ones in Sheriton?" he asks, eyes wide with shock. "You think they bought their supplies from my shop?!"

Putting a hand on the shopkeeper's shoulder, Logan gives him a wry smile. "If it turns out they did, it won't be any fault of yours. And if they'd bought it elsewhere we may not have had such good security footage to look at; you may well have saved the day!"

This seems to help Mr Alexander come to terms with the awful situation he finds himself in. But it is clear that he isn't comfortable with it.

Handing Catherine the cd, he says, "Perhaps you will let me know if it helps you to catch them? It would help, I think."

"Of course I will," Catherine assures the man. "And if it does and there's a reward-"

But Mr Alexander looks horrified and shakes his head fiercely. "No! Never! I will not profit from all those deaths – and to think I sold them the rope..."

Despite their attempts to console the man, Mr Alexander says that if any reward is due to him then it must go to the fund he has seen advertised on the TV for the families.

"I feel bad for him," Catherine admits as Logan pulls the Range Rover away from the shop. "It's not like he knew what they wanted it for."

"Would you feel any differently?" Logan asks, already knowing the answer.

"About the reward money...?" Catherine doesn't really need to consider her answer but takes her time to put it in the right words. "No. Even if I'd been fresh out of foster care without a penny to my name, I couldn't have taken blood money. But I wouldn't have blamed him if he had – it wasn't his fault."

"Let's hope that footage proves as useful as you think it might. Could you actually tell what taxi firm it was?" Logan asks, not at all sure that he could.

"There's a couple that it could be," Catherine admits. "I'll just have to go through their logs and see what I can find."

"Why don't you just call them and ask – wouldn't that be simpler?"

"You'd think so wouldn't you? But what if Wade uses another name – something like Cherish Lovett?" she suggests with a raised brow. "I would recognise that, but I can't expect the taxi firms to go through their records looking for half a dozen different names. And even if they did, they're unlikely to do so as carefully as I would."

Conceding the point, Logan tries to come to terms with the fact that his wife regularly breaks the law – though he also has to admit that she's damned good at it!

"Could we call in to The Lovett – I just want to see Travis and the girls," she explains when Logan turns briefly to look at her.

"No problem." And he turns the car onto a dual carriageway that should get them there in about half an hour. "Have you heard from Travis today?"

"I phoned this morning before we left out," Catherine nods. "He sounded...sort of weird," she frowns, not sure why she thought he'd sounded that way. "Don't ask me why, but it was like I thought he was going to tell me something and then he didn't."

"You think he's hiding something?" Logan asks, thinking it unlikely that Travis would do any such thing.

"No. Well...maybe," Catherine muses, her mind evidently not made up. "I'll feel better once I've seen him face to face – I don't think Travis has your ability to hide what you're thinking. You have a very good poker face," she tells him, turning to stare at his profile consideringly.

"Somehow, that doesn't sound like a compliment..." Logan frowns. "...though it has come in handy when doing deals. I've managed to pull off some good ones in my time," he smiles smugly.

"Ha!" Catherine laughs, remembering what she'd thought of him when they had first met in Arthur Kingsley's office. "You look just like you did back when we first met – Mr High-and-mighty-Sayers," she laughs again, as Logan looks taken aback.

"I have never been the High-and-mighty sort," he denies indignantly in his best Etonian voice. "I enjoy winning – there's no shame in that!"

"So do I..." Catherine admits, "...I won't settle for anything less. And, to be honest, I'm glad you don't either. I like that ruthless streak you have in you – it's sexy," she smiles, then laughs when Logan squirms uncomfortably in his seat.

"We'll talk about 'sexy' later," he frowns, but can't stop his lips from tilting up at the corners. "We'll be at the hotel in another couple of minutes."

Turning off the dual carriageway and onto a busy 'A' road, Logan drives swiftly but surely until they pull into The Lovett Hotel car park.

There are news vans present, and Catherine fears that something has happened to Travis or the girls.

"Come on," Logan takes her arm and quickly guides Catherine through a throng of people in the hotel lobby. "Don't stop or look around – I think they may have found out about Caroline's abduction."

It was bound to happen. As much as the police have tried to keep it quiet, Caroline's disappearance is big news and someone may have sold the story to the press.

Keying in the lift's access code, they press to summon it and thankfully it arrives seconds later. And not a moment too soon – an alert newshound had tried shoving a microphone in her face to ask questions just as the lift doors were closing.

"I know they have a job to do, but they're like rats pouring out of a sewer," Catherine grimaces.

Stepping out of the lift into the penthouse, Catherine goes straight into Travis's arms. "You must be worried to death – I know this is the last thing Frank wanted to happen!"

Momentarily needing the physical contact, Travis doesn't pull away and knows that this show of emotion is rare indeed for Catherine.

"It's ok, Caroline will be home soon," Travis whispers softly. "She has to come home soon, we can't live without her."

Standing back, watching their emotions bond their strength and love together, Logan feels nothing but pride for the woman he loves and gratitude that Catherine has chosen to share her life with him.

"She's still ok..." Catherine pulls back from Travis to look him in the eyes, "...I feel her connection all the time – I just wish I could bring her home to you."

Stroking her cheek, Travis nods and smiles, "You will, Catherine – you're not ready to let her go any more than I am. Caroline is a very special part of us, isn't she?"

Stepping forward, Logan puts a supportive hand to his brother-in-law's shoulder and gives it a squeeze. "She's working all hours to get Caroline back..." Logan tells him, "...but Catherine was worried about you today, she had a feeling that something was amiss?"

Looking at Catherine, Travis just frowns quizzically and guides her to take a seat on one of the large settees. "Did you get some kind of...image, or something," he asks hesitantly.

"Not exactly..." Catherine replies still holding his hand, "...it was more like...a void...a space that you didn't fill in when we spoke on the phone earlier. You sounded wrong. Just...wrong..."

Shaking his head and looking at her in wonder, Travis eventually smiles. "I didn't want to upset you over the phone," he begins hesitantly, the thought of telling Caroline's sister that his old ex-fiancée is trying to get back into his life not one he has been relishing.

Swallowing down her fear, Catherine feels her heart skip several beats. "Just tell me, Travis. Whatever it is, just get it out fast."

Nodding his understanding, Travis takes a breath then dives right in. "Cherish came to the hotel last night and made it clear, without putting it into the exact words, that she wants to be back in my life. She believes herself to be in love with me," he admits quietly. "But more than that...I believe Cherish is hoping that if she keeps Caroline out of the picture, I will love her the way I used to."

He watches Catherine blanch at his words and sees the pain they cause her. "But she can't just step into Caroline's life like that – how could she possibly believe that she can?" Catherine is horrified, shocked by the simplicity of the woman's twisted mind. "But if she does believe it, if she truly sees her future with you in it, Caroline is running out of time. What did you say to Wade – you didn't just blow her off, did you?"

Letting out a deep sigh, Travis shakes his head. "No, much as I wanted to, I tried to gently dissuade her – but it's like she's living in the past. In her world the last 18 years never happened."

Thinking better on her feet, Catherine gets up to pace the room. "Do you think she's still on her meds?"

"If she is, I'd have to guess that she isn't taking them properly," Travis speculates thoughtfully. "Sometimes she sounded lucid, right in the here and now – but at others, she was back to when we were a couple...all loving and hopeful, as sweet as she used to be," he smiles sadly.

"You're not getting soft on her, are you?" Catherine asks, a glint of steel in her eyes.

"No – but I can't not care about her at all, Catherine. I loved her once; Cherish was a very big part of my life, the one I thought I would plan my future with – so don't ask me to just turn my back on her and walk away," Travis explains, pleading for her understanding.

For what seems like an eternity, Catherine stands looking at Travis like she can't believe what she's hearing; but then her mind clears and she can hear her sister's voice telling her, *He wouldn't be the man I love if he were able to do that. Help him, Catherine – help Cherish to let him go.*

"Ok, but if she hurts you…" A tear slides from Catherine's eyes as they refocus on Travis. "Caroline just told me that you wouldn't be the man she loves if you could do that…" closing her eyes, she swipes at the tell-tale tears and steels herself, "…and she wants me to help Cherish to let you go."

Standing, Travis moves to take Catherine in his arms again and thanks her with all his heart. "Together, Catherine, we will bring Caroline home!"

CHAPTER FIFTEEN

"I'm so proud of what you did today," Logan tells Catherine, and leans over to take her hand after parking the Range Rover back at Lakelands.

"Hearing Caroline's voice in my head like that...it's hard, Logan," Catherine admits, her eyes pooling with deep emotions. "She's so close, I feel her right inside my heart...yet I can't find her. And I'm terrified that I never will...that I'll fail again!"

"Hush..." Logan croons as he pulls her to him, "...you never failed your mother, and you will not fail your sister."

"But what if I do?" Catherine pulls away from him, looking at Logan with no defences in place to hide her fear. "What if Caroline dies because I couldn't keep my head together enough to make sense of the clues right in front of me? There has to be something I'm not seeing – something I haven't yet done!"

Pulling the cd of the hardware shop's security footage out of his jacket pocket, Logan holds it out to Catherine. "Here's something we haven't done yet," he tells her. "And you might want to take note of that little word 'we'," he emphasises with a raised brow. "You are not on your own in this – all of us are trying to find Caroline – we love her too!"

For the next few hours, Catherine, Logan, Emma and Linda all work on the case. Inspector Frank Harper lets them know that he believes he is making progress with the arson investigation. A home improvements shop had become suspicious of a customer buying large quantities of turpentine and had contacted the police with the details. The customer had been a male and sounded very like the man who had bought the rope from the hardware shop.

Capturing an image of the man from the cd, Catherine emails it across to the inspector and just has to hope that it will prove useful.

"He's worried there's going to be another arson attack," Catherine tells them after getting off the phone with Frank.

"Let's just hope we find them before they get the chance," Emma replies, her fingers still dancing across her laptop's keyboard.

When Catherine's personal mobile rings she is startled and looks around the room, somewhat bewildered – the only people who would normally call her are Adrianne, Caroline and everyone else in the room. Ruling out the obvious, her mind goes to either Caroline or Adrianne.

Watching his wife take out her mobile, Logan is concerned when he watches her face go pale.

"What is it?" he asks, moving to her side.

"It's Robert," Catherine replies, still looking at the name on the small screen.

"Hadn't you better answer him?"

Pressing the answer button, Catherine just about manages to say, "Hello."

Watching Catherine listening to her brother-in-law is very frustrating for Logan as all she is doing in reply is nodding her head.

"We'll be there right away," she tells Robert, finally managing to speak. "Is Adrianne really alright?" When Robert assures her that her sister is in labour but very excited, Catherine begins to relax. "Ok...that's ok then," and she lets out a shaky breath and gives Logan a tremulous smile.

"She's in labour!" Logan's smile is much brighter than Catherine's and he picks her up to spin her around. "Finally, the last one is about to arrive!"

"You maniac!" Catherine bats at his chest when Logan eventually puts her down, then covers her mouth and runs to the nearest bathroom.

Following hot on her heels, Logan watches as she wretches into the toilet. "Christ, I'm sorry. I just got carried away."

But Catherine is smiling when her head finally emerges. "I think it was all the nervous tension I've been prone to lately." Swilling her mouth with hands full of cold water over the sink, Catherine splashes some on her face and feels a lot better. "Come on, let's go and meet our nephew."

Much quicker than her sisters, Adrianne gives birth to a strapping son in just under an hour. Weighing in at 8lbs 6oz, it hadn't been an easy birthing but it had been fast, the doctor announced; but added that mother and baby were both doing well.

"Oh dad," Catherine hugs her father and then Erin, all the while struggling not to cry.

Everyone is thinking 'if only Caroline were here' but none of them voice the thought out loud. This is

Adrianne's special day, they must be happy for her and for Robert.

But when they are invited into the delivery room to meet their nephew and grandson, Catherine and Tom find Adrianne shedding a few quiet tears of her own.

"Isn't he wonderful?" Adrianne moves the blanket to show off her son, her lower lip trembling badly. "He's Matthew Robert Kingsley," she announces, then offers him up to his granddad.

Grinning proudly, Tom looks down at the black haired little boy with the bright blue eyes. "He's a handsome little fellow," Tom declares, smiling over at his son-in-law. "You'll have your hands full now, lad!"

Looking bemused by it all, Robert smiles and nods wordlessly, still clinging to Adrianne's hand.

"I think he's still in shock..." Adrianne chuckles, bringing Robert's knuckles up to her lips, "...it all happened rather suddenly. One minute we were sitting down to supper and the next my waters broke and pandemonium ensued. We only just made it in time!"

"That is thee understatement of the year!" Robert proclaims having finally found his voice. "There was no time to call an ambulance – one minute her waters break...the next Adrianne is in full blown labour and the baby is on his way. I swear..." Robert breaths a huge sigh of relief, and looks at Logan as a fellow recent dad, "...I thought I was going to have to deliver him myself in the car. I'm telling you, I've never been so scared in all my life!"

Clapping him on the back, Logan leans down to shake Robert's hand. "Well, you've done it once, the next two should be a piece of cake!" And everyone, including Adrianne, laughs at Robert's look of alarm.

"You did say you wanted three in quick succession," Catherine reminds him, and looks at Adrianne to see if she's still as keen on the idea.

"Absolutely," Adrianne declares, taking her son as Tom hands him back. Her eyes are dreamy, looking adoringly into the chubby little face. "I want at least 3," she smiles, and dips her head to kiss Matthew's forehead.

Opening and closing his mouth like a guppy, Robert can only stare at his wife until his eyes, too, become adoring as he takes in the lovely picture Adrianne makes with their son in her arms.

"I'm glad she didn't have a prolonged labour," Catherine tells Logan during the drive home. "Adrianne had the worst time with morning sickness; she deserved to catch a break!"

"I don't think it was all plain sailing from what Robert told me," Logan remarks casually. "Apparently Adrianne needed a lot of stitches – the doctors said the size of the baby plus the speed of the labour didn't give Adrianne's body time to adjust."

Frowning over at him, Catherine looks worried. "Did Robert say if they were worried about any future births?"

"Not exactly, but they did tell him that they would be monitoring Adrianne much more carefully towards the end of any future pregnancy," Logan explains. "Evidently, babies generally get bigger the more you have... so..."

With a shrug of his broad shoulders, Logan leaves that thought hanging in the air.

"Bloody hell – bigger than 8lbs 6oz – she'll never manage it!" Catherine declares with a grimace of sympathy.

Chuckling deeply, Logan pulls into Lakelands and feels the peace of home spread through him. It always gives him the feeling that here he can do anything, cope with anything – such is its restorative effect on his psyche.

Taking her hand as they walk up to the grand house, Logan smiles down at her with love in his eyes. "You know, our boys were smaller because they were twins..." he observes musingly, "...but if we had a single baby, who knows how big it would be."

Shocked and somewhat appalled by the thought, Catherine pulls Logan to a halt. "What the hell are you saying? I thought that was it, two for the price of one – no more, never, nada – now you sound like you're already looking forward to another one!"

Stepping to her, putting his arms around Catherine and holding her head to his heart, Logan rests his cheek on the top of her head.

"Our boys are wonderful," he declares with wonder in his rich deep voice.

"But...?"

"There is no 'but', not really. I suppose it was seeing Robert and Adrianne – I'm just getting the male equivalence of broody," he chuckles, though Catherine is sure she heard the longing behind his words.

"It's time for the boys' feed," Catherine reminds him. "Let's go up."

Never able to imagine herself as a mother, Catherine went through her entire pregnancy fearful that she wouldn't be very good at it.

Memories of her mother's love had been shattered by witnessing her torture murder. And, as for foster care, the parents who took her into their families were not examples that she would ever want to follow.

But now, as she holds Adam to her breast, Catherine feels a love she had never suspected that she was capable of, such is the overwhelming need to care for and protect her boys. *But another baby? How would we cope, for one thing? I need to work to keep my sanity – I'll go crazy if I don't stretch myself mentally. I don't want to become that sullen or waspish person that I used to be.*

Almost asleep in her arms, Adam relinquishes her breast having taken his fill and, after giving him a kiss and a brief cuddle, they swap the boys over.

Now Andrew latches on to her other breast and Catherine smiles down into his beautiful brown eyes – so exactly like his daddy's though not quite as deep in colour.

Both boys had been born with blue eyes, as all babies are, but gradually they have darkened and look as though they might go as brown as Logan's eyes are.

Stroking his head, Catherine watches her son blink up at her as if memorising her face to take to his dreams, and feels her heart ache with love.

Maybe it wouldn't be so bad; I wouldn't be so scared all the time for one thing. Jesus – finding out I was pregnant had been the biggest shock, just the thought of having something growing inside me...

But that had changed quickly, the feeling of her boys moving and stretching becoming a wonder to Catherine and Logan alike.

Looking up at him now, Catherine watches as Logan rubs Adam's back having laid him over his shoulder with a towel under him.

"You look so damned good at that," Catherine smiles contentedly, moving slowly back and forth in her rocking chair. "A real pro."

"You look amazing," he smiles, the love in his eyes so deep and sincere.

Hesitantly, Catherine finds herself telling him to just give her some time. "I need to be sure, Logan. I don't want to risk everything we have by making a snap decision – is that ok?"

His smile couldn't get any brighter as Logan reaches out to cup her face. "There's no rush – we'll do whatever you decide. You've already given me so much, Catherine – and I'm not just talking about our sons."

Precious; everything they have between them is so very precious.

CHAPTER SIXTEEN

Pacing the basement of a derelict paper mill on the outskirts of town, Cherish Wade is fighting a battle that will decide Caroline's fate.

She's standing between you and all you've ever wanted; get rid of her! The voice is insistent, and sometimes Cherish comes face to face with it in the guise of a woman not unlike herself, but a little older and with bitterness etched in every line of her face.

"No! Not yet!" Cherish stands her ground, but feels it shaking beneath her feet. "Travis would never forgive me-"

Travis will never know...and he'll be yours, all yours. He'll never think of her again once you take your rightful place at his side. He was yours before he was ever hers, the sly voice cajoles reasonably.

Caroline watches in horror, knowing that she must not draw attention to herself while her captor is so deranged. *Catherine? Catherine...can you hear me? Please, Catherine, I don't think I have much time left, Cherish is becoming more and more unstable. I think she's going to kill me...*

Hearing her sister as clearly as if she had been in the same room with her, Catherine stops suddenly in the process of holding a mug of coffee to her lips.

The vague look in Catherine's eyes causes Emma to frown and ask, "You ok? Catherine...?"

But Catherine is seeing and hearing what Caroline is seeing and hearing and it is shocking to behold.

"She's losing it!" Catherine declares suddenly. *I'm with you, Caroline...I can hear you, and I can see what you see. Look around the room for me; let me see where you are.*

Staying quiet, Emma has moved to stand beside Catherine aware that she is experiencing some kind of psychic phenomena. But she becomes worried when Catherine doesn't appear to be coming out of it.

Oh Catherine, it's such a relief to hear you – I'm so sorry, I don't know how I let this happen. My girls, my babies...and Travis...I won't let this be the end, Catherine. Please, don't let this be the end...

Feeling their connection so strong and so clear, Catherine tries to give her sister some much needed reassurance.

Never! Now do as I asked and take a slow look around the room. That's it...ok...no, go back...look to your right...yes, there in the corner. Turpentine! So he did buy it for her, Catherine realises.

Who did? Caroline asks.

We don't know who he is yet, but Frank and Sloane are looking into it. We got a good photo of him from the shop's security footage – they'll soon pick him up and then we'll come get you. Just don't give up, Caroline – I'm right there with you.

Feeling her sister's fear, Catherine has to project a strong belief that they are close so that Caroline doesn't realise how scared of failing she really is.

It's alright, Catherine, I'm holding on. Just keep doing what you're doing and we'll be together soon. I believe in you, Catherine – I love you, sis.

When the contact is broken and Catherine begins to see her surroundings, instead of the basement where her sister is being held, she comes face to face with Logan.

"There you are," he croons with deep relief as he watches her eyes regain their focus. "Are you alright?"

Nodding, Catherine puts her arms about his neck and her head on his shoulder. For a wonderful moment they just hold each other and breathe in the familiar scent of their soul mate until their world settles and rights itself.

"I'm ok, but Caroline is running out of time," she tells Logan, and looks up to include a very worried looking Emma. "Wade is barking, she's talking to herself and working up to killing Caroline, I think."

"Oh God!" Emma gasps, her eyes going wide.

"And the turpentine was there," Catherine turns back to Logan. "I could see it, bottles of it in the corner of the room. I think Frank is right, she's planning another fire!"

"I think we need to call Frank and Sloane, get them up to date and on side for whatever comes next," Emma states decisively.

Looking at her husband, who is nodding in agreement, Catherine turns her gaze back to Emma and says, "Call them, will you?" Turning back to Logan, she reiterates her sister's fears. "Caroline doesn't think she has much time left; from what I saw and heard of Wade's behaviour, I'd have to agree."

"Did you see anything that might help to identify where Caroline is being held?"

"No...though...now I think about it, it didn't look like a house basement," Catherine frowns, trying to pull back the memory. "I can't think why, but it just didn't look right – it had an industrial feel to it."

"Ok, Frank and Sloane are on their way," Emma turns and walks back to them. "Are you ok?"

"I'm fine – it's Caroline who's in trouble," Catherine sighs heavily, rubbing her eyes in an effort to clear the ache behind them.

"What do you want to do now?" Logan asks.

"I wish I knew," Catherine shakes her head slowly. "But I think Linda needs to sit in when Frank and Sloane get here – she might be able to give us a clue as to what's happening with Wade."

"Ok." Logan pushes up to his feet and walks over to the kettle, switching it on. "I need a strong black coffee – anyone else?"

Both Emma and Catherine give a nod, then Catherine walks over to the whiteboards and begins running through the information pinned there.

There has to be something we've missed. Where is she holding Caroline? Looking at a large street map of Sheriton, Catherine begins circling relevant buildings. *Ok, that's the school, the cinema, Wade's current rented house and her parent's old place – what else?*

"What about your sister's hotel – The Lovett," Emma suggests, watching what Catherine is about. "That's where she took Caroline from, and it's where Travis still lives...so..."

"Your right," Catherine takes her pen and circles The Lovett Hotel. "If Wade is holding Caroline in somewhere industrial, where would it be?"

Emma points to a small industrial estate on the outskirts of Sheriton and Catherine circles it.

"There are some smaller, stand alone buildings on this side of the town," Emma points to show Catherine where she means. "Not all the floors are in use though."

Catherine turns to Emma and frowns quizzically.

"I mean, take this building..." and she points to a large structure that appears to have a considerable footprint, "...there are a lot of different companies working out of it. They rent a floor or even half of one if they don't need that much space – it's cheaper than renting a whole separate building."

"How do you know it isn't fully occupied?"

"Because I've been checking out possible places that Wade could be holding Caroline – just in case," Emma adds with a shrug. And moving closer to Catherine, she whispers, "I did a little hacking and got the tenant list. The first and third floors are empty and the building does have a basement."

"That's good work," Catherine smiles and nods. "Did you find any other possibles?"

"Yes, there's a derelict paper mill here, and an old office block further along here," Emma points, and Catherine circles them in a different colour. "On the industrial estate, there are a lot of vacant units..." Emma purses her lips and sighs, "...the recession seems to have put a lot of small manufacturers out of business. I'll print out the list I've got on my laptop – I'm sorry to say, there are a lot of possible places she could be."

"Ok, let's put the list up here next to the map – the dynamic duo may have some ideas."

Emma lets out chuckle, which turns into a real laugh when the dynamic duo themselves walk into the office. Leaning to whisper in Catherine's ear, Emma asks, "So, which one do you see as Batman?"

Finding herself amused at such a perilous time, Catherine finds some of her pent up tension easing.

"Hi Frank, Sloane," Catherine greets the two police officers.

As Logan has just finished making a round of coffees he offers the new arrivals a cup.

"Thanks," Frank and Sloane say together, and both turn to look at Emma who has to stifle a giggle.

"Ok, we just need Linda," Catherine states to no one in particular. "Just give me a minute."

While they wait for her return, Frank and Sloane walk over to the whiteboards to see what's been put together.

Sloane stands in front of the street map studying the circles and nods. When he feels Emma move to his side he holds out a hand to point to a couple of the circled buildings, "These are probable's. The ones over here are possible's as they are further away and would require transport to move Mrs Lovett – as far as we know, Wade doesn't drive," but he turns a questioning look on Emma for confirmation.

Shaking her head, Emma confirms that Wade had never passed her driving test. "But she did have a number of lessons before she was locked up, so..." She shrugs, pursing her lips.

"And we still haven't found Mrs Lovett's car," Sloane frowns. "Ok, so the possible's move up the list."

The office door opens and Linda comes in followed by Catherine. "As you all know, Linda is a qualified Psychologist with many years experience – not in this field, but I'm sure you'll agree her insight will be invaluable." And looking straight at Detective Sloane Shivers she challenges him to say otherwise.

When he doesn't, Catherine crosses the room to pull up a chair for Linda but the older woman tells her not to trouble. "I'm happy standing," Linda smiles.

"Ok then..." Catherine sits on the edge of her desk and holds a hand out to Emma, "...you start. Bring everyone up to date going back from the school fire and working up to Caroline's disappearance."

Swallowing her hot coffee in a panicked gulp, Emma has to cough a couple of times before she can speak. "The Mosbry Senior School was burned down using a petrol accelerant and rope was used to tie off the exits, trapping the occupants inside. The exact same MO was used in the burning down of the cinema the following night – the rope has been forensically confirmed as being the exact same type," she tells them in a clinically distant voice.

"We know that both Wade and Travis Lovett went to school together at Mosbry and, apparently, the cinema was one of their favourite dating venues. We've tried to ascertain any other likely targets, but Travis doesn't remember anywhere else that would have been significant to Wade other than The Lovett Hotel itself," and Emma looks disturbed by this thought.

"Logan managed to trace where the rope was purchased from. We extracted a photo from the hardware shop's security disc," and she points to the image of a man pinned to a whiteboard. "A taxi that the man got into after leaving the shop was identified and the firm contacted. They got back to us and confirmed that a woman, fitting Wade's description, was a passenger in that same taxi and that both passengers were dropped off in close proximity to Wade's rented house – though not at the exact address," she sighs.

"The fare was paid in cash and the taxi was a flag down, so no record of a booking. The driver called in to say that he'd picked up a fare on Laxton Street and gave the hardware shop's address as his destination – so, we know that purchasing the rope was their sole intention"

Picking up her mug, Emma takes a much needed drink of her coffee then begins again.

"More recently a large amount of bottled turps was purchased from a different hardware shop and the owner reported the purchase as suspicious in light of the recent arson attacks. When we looked at the security footage from that shop we were able to identify the man as being the same one who had purchased the rope."

Looking hopefully at Frank and Sloane she asks, "Do you know who he is yet?"

Sloane shakes his head, "No, but we've got beat cops showing the picture around in the hopes that someone will recognise him."

"We've been looking at footage and stills from both crime scenes in the hopes that we'll spot the perp at both of them, but no luck thus far."

Then Emma hesitates and looks to Catherine. "There's more, but I think we should cut to the chase and get to what happened this morning. Catherine, do you want to explain?"

Closing her eyes, Catherine can feel all eyes on her and the feeling of dread that she's been pushing down, rises up causing her to swallow hard.

Blowing out a long breath, Catherine opens her eyes but remains seated on the edge of her desk. "You all know that Caroline and I are identical twins and that we have a 'connection'," and she mimes quotation marks in the air and watches the small group nod as one. "Well, this morning Caroline's voice came into my head so clearly she could have been talking to me in the same room." Looking at the faces now turned to her, Catherine looks for signs of disbelief but finds none.

"It's never been that clear before – I could actually see and hear everything that Caroline was looking at and listening to – it was damned scary," she tails off, remembering Wade's frantic ramblings.

"Did you see anything that could identify where she's being held?" Frank asks hopefully.

But Catherine is shaking her head. "Not that I remember – but I did get the feeling that it wasn't a domestic basement. You know, the kind you get in old houses," she clarifies.

"What makes you say that?" Sloane narrows his eyes at her.

"I don't know exactly, it was more an impression, I think, of somewhere industrial." Catherine holds her hands palms upwards and lets them fall into her lap. "But what I did see, and as clearly as if they were in this very room, was the bottles of turps stashed in a corner of the room on the concrete floor."

"Concrete...you didn't mention that," Sloane picks her up on the small detail. "Was it rough, like a domestic dwelling might have, or was it smooth and polished like a factory or an office building might use?"

Blinking and frowning at him, Catherine tries to pull back the image. "I think you've got something there – that's what made me think of somewhere industrial – it had a smooth, professional finish." Catherine continues to frown, trying desperately to pull back even more details. "There's something else, I just can't put my finger on it, damn it!"

Having a near photographic memory, Catherine isn't used to struggling to remember details and becomes distressed by her inability.

Rubbing at her forehead, she has to fight back the embarrassing tears that are gathering behind her closed eyelids. "Why can't I do this? I can remember books I read years ago, inane facts that are no good to anyone, so why can't I remember what I saw just an hour ago?"

Crossing to her, Linda puts a hand on Catherine's shoulder and says, "Because this involves your emotions, and fear is probably interfering with your usually excellent memory." When Catherine raises her eyes to look at Linda, she can see the desperation in them. "Try working through the memory methodically – what did you see first, or did you hear Caroline's voice first?"

"It was her voice – she was terrified," Catherine recalls, and the memory begins to come together in her mind. "She was calling to me, desperate for me to find her – I could hear Wade arguing with herself, and then I could see her, like I was in the same room," Catherine tells them, her tone portraying the astonishment she still felt at that.

When she falls silent, Linda gives her a quiet prompt, "Did you see Caroline – is she alright?"

Drawing her brows together, Catherine shakes her head, "I wasn't separate, I was looking through Caroline's eyes and I could feel her fear. It was so intense; she knows she's going to die..."

A sob breaks free from Catherine's increasingly tight airway, her breathing becoming laboured, and Logan is at her side in an instant.

CHAPTER SEVENTEEN

"Enough now!" Logan declares, taking Catherine into his arms and standing between her and the group of people watching on.

For a blessed moment, Catherine allows herself to sink into him, Logan's strong arms giving her a place of refuge like no other. But Caroline needs her, and Catherine has never been a coward.

Turning her head into his solid chest, she places a kiss there and then looks up into Logan's very worried brown eyes. "I can do this – I just need a minute, that's all." But she loves when his arms tighten about her before finally letting her go, though Logan doesn't move from her side.

Looking at Linda, Catherine continues, "Wade appeared to be arguing with herself – I think she's teetering on the edge of giving in to whatever the voice in her head is telling her. It's difficult to know exactly – listening to only one side of a conversation might be misleading – but I definitely heard her say that 'Travis would never forgive her' and that's when Caroline realised that Wade could really kill her."

Looking up at Logan, Catherine's bottom lip trembles tellingly, "All she could think of was her babies, her girls, and Travis...how he would manage without her..."

Reaching for her hand, Logan gives it an encouraging squeeze and continues to hold it when Catherine continues.

"I don't know why I can recall Caroline's feelings so acutely and not what I was seeing through her eyes," Catherine sighs heavily and again looks to Linda for answers.

"I believe it's the same thing that blocked your connection to Caroline in the beginning," Linda smiles ruefully. "Your emotions are so heightened by the fear of losing Caroline that they are taking precedence over everything else. The fact that you were able to communicate with Caroline so clearly this time, may be because of Caroline's own determination, her desperate need to tell you that time is growing short."

"So, she bulldozed her way in?" Catherine asks, then nods her understanding. "Yes...that's pretty much how it felt – like she burst into my head and I had no choice but to listen.”

Having listened closely to the unusual discussion, Sloane decides to ask Catherine to do something that could help to break the case wide open – though he looks cautiously at Logan before voicing his request.

“What about trying again – contact Caroline, see if you can get a more detailed visual of the room she's in?” he suggests bravely.

Even his boss, Inspector Frank Harper, looks at Shivers like he's an insensitive clod, but then his eyes betray the fact that he's considering the suggestion.

“Are you crazy?” Logan stands to attention at Catherine's side, his stance protective in the extreme. “Can't you tell that she's had enough – or doesn't that matter to you?!” he accuses, his angry eyes spitting daggers in Sloane Shivers' direction.

That the man doesn't shrivel into a gibbering mass on the floor is to his credit, and Sloane even manages to stand his ground. “Would you rather Catherine has to deal with her sister's death?” he asks, his voice deceptively quiet. “And not just her death, but the fact that she might have been able to save her...but didn't.”

A collective gasp punctuates the brief silence, then Catherine steps forward. “You don't need to make me feel any worse than I already do," she tells Sloane, just as quietly. "It won't help — if anything it's my emotions that are getting in the way. I need to approach this differently — just give me a minute," and she walks to the whiteboards, looking at all the information they've gathered, the photos of the burned out buildings and the number of lives that had been lost.

I can do this! I want to do this to give those victims and their families' closure, but even more important right now, I need to bring my sister home!

"Ok, I'm ready!"

The thought of trying to make a connection with Caroline under the watchful gaze of an audience is very off-putting. Sitting at her desk, Catherine closes her eyes and tries to tune out their presence.

"Caroline...can you hear me?" she asks, not realising that she is saying the words out loud.

"Catherine...oh, Catherine...I can hear you, are you near, are you coming to get me?"

"We're trying, sis'," Catherine tries to sound reassuring. "Have you got your eyes closed — I can't see like I could before?"

Frank and Sloane look at each other and give a sigh of frustration.

"She put tape over my eyes and I felt her wrapping some more round my wrists and ankles, though they were already tied," Caroline tells her, and then her voice cracks. "Catherine, I heard her talking to someone – not the voice," she clarifies quickly, "this someone actually answered her, I heard him."

"Him?!" Catherine asks abruptly. "Did you hear what they said...did she call him by name?"

"I...no...I don't think so..."

"Think, Caroline!" Catherine demands. "We know she's working with someone but we haven't got a name – try to remember."

"They weren't near me – it sounded echoey, like they were standing in a very large empty room," Caroline recalls.

"So you don't think you're in a basement?" Catherine asks, surprised by the thought.

"I'm not sure, but if I am it must be a big one with at least one separate room – the one I'm in," Caroline tells her. "Catherine..." Caroline's voice has become little more than a whisper, but is clear enough for Catherine to hear her, "...I need to know that you'll help Travis with the girls...and that...and that, you won't let them forget me..."

Catherine is shaken by the utter despair in her sister's voice and feels her profound desolation. "Stop that! You can't give up! Do you hear me – you can't give up! I'm coming for you; we'll raise our children together!"

Emma has to stifle a sob with a hand to her mouth, and Sloane moves in to offer comfort. "We can't let this happen," she murmurs tearfully, and the arm around Emma's waist tightens momentarily.

"We'll get her back," Sloane tells her, hoping desperately that they can.

All Catherine can hear now is her sister's sobs. "Stop snivelling, Caroline!" she demands roughly, trying to snap her out of it. "If you want to get home to Travis and your girls, you'll have to do better than this. Now tell me what you can hear – is Wade still with you?"

Feeling her sister check her emotions, Catherine tries to hold her ground when Caroline says, "I'd like to see you do any better in my place!" Then Catherine laughs and the strain between the sisters eases.

"You're right, I'd be a pathetic puddle on the floor if I were in your shoes," Catherine admits. "But you're stronger than that – your girls need you, Caroline...Travis needs you."

Struggling to take a deep breath, Caroline tries to focus on her family. "Ok, just give me a second to think. She isn't here – or, at least, I can't hear her. I can usually hear her shoes clip-clopping on the floor when she's nearby, so I think she's gone out somewhere."

"Ok. Alright then, let's try to work this out," Catherine murmurs inanely. "What can you smell – can you make out anything distinctive?"

Caroline sniffs the air, trying to identify the smell that had made her feel nauseous when she'd first woken up in this place. "It isn't as strong now, or maybe I've just become accustomed to it – but when I first woke up I could smell something caustic – something sharp that burned my nose."

"Like cleaning fluid?" Catherine asks.

"Well...sort of...I suppose," Caroline doesn't sound convinced. "I just don't know, Catherine – but it was so strong I could almost taste it, at first – it made me feel sick."

"Ok, we've got something to work on," Catherine assures her. "We'll start looking for businesses that used that type of fluid. They're obviously not working there now, so maybe they went out of business recently – hence the strong odour."

"Catherine...will you let dad and Adrianne know that I'm thinking of them – that I love them," Caroline asks, the sadness back in her voice.

"Are you kidding, they've been demanding updates regularly," Catherine tells her. "But I'll let them know what you said – they love you, too. We all do," and Catherine has to slam the door tight shut on the tears that are threatening to overwhelm her. "Let me know if you hear or see anything else," she tells Caroline. "The sooner I get working on this the sooner we'll get you back home."

Neither sister wants to break their link, but in the end, it is Caroline who closes her mind off.

"Oh, Jesus!" Catherine slumps forward with her hands covering her face, bereft now that her connection with Caroline has been severed.

Don't give up, Caroline – I won't let this be the end. I need you, too...

"Cleaning fluid...?" Emma asks when Catherine raises her head.

Nodding, Catherine brutally shuts off her emotions and gets her brain into gear. "Yes, Caroline could smell something caustic – something that burned her nose and made her feel sick," she recollects for those who weren't privy to the other side of the conversation.

"I'll get a list of the businesses that have recently moved or ceased trading," Emma tells her, and strides across the room to sit behind her laptop.

"We'll do the same, and try to get an ID on this man," Frank points to the picture of the man known to be working with Cherish Wade.

Frank and Sloane take their leave and, after Catherine thanks her for sitting in, so does Linda.

When Logan moves to stand by her side, Catherine turns into his solid strength and finds her own strength building from his.

"I need to see our boys," Catherine looks up, the necessity to feel their sons safe in her arms clear to Logan.

"We can take some time out," he assures her, and looks over to Emma who is already deep in concentration and the task she's set herself.

Walking into the nursery, Catherine stands at the end of Adam's cot and watches the little boy sleeping soundly. "Any other time he'd be awake now, demanding to be fed," she smiles ruefully. "Now, when my arms ache to hold him, he's flat out."

Logan lets out a soft chuckle, and they move on to Andrew's cot. Leaning down, Catherine strokes his fluffy hair and his soft chubby cheeks. "I wouldn't dare touch Adam like this – he wakes too easily, and it's still early yet for their feed."

But having said that Catherine still looks hopefully across at Adam, almost willing him to wake.

"They're safe, Catherine," Logan assures her, knowing that her fear for Caroline is being reflected onto their sons. "They are loved and they are happy, and we won't let any harm come to them."

"But-"

"No..." Logan puts a finger to her lips, stifling what he knows will be her anxious 'what ifs', "...our boys are not in any danger, and you borrowing trouble is not going to help anyone – least of all Caroline."

She knows he's right – Logan usually is, Catherine acknowledges with a sigh. "Ok, we'd better get back to work. I just...I needed to see them, just to be sure."

Drawing her into his arms, Logan kisses her tenderly. "I love you, Catherine, with all my heart and soul. And, whatever happens, we'll get through this together."

But after several hours of coming up empty, Catherine becomes desperate.

CHAPTER EIGHTEEN

"We need Farraday," Catherine states, her hands agitatedly pushing back through her short blonde hair. "Caroline can't show me where she is, but maybe Farraday can go there?!"

"Go there...?" Emma frowns, confused.

With her arms expressively flailing in the air, Catherine turns to her colleague and tries to explain. "Yes, though not physically," she tells her, and watches Emma's frown deepen. "Christ, don't you remember me telling you how he walks through his visions? He's practically there in person!" Catherine sighs heavily, her face a picture of exasperation.

"I remember you telling me something of the sort," Emma nods uncertainly. "So you think he might be able to do this 'vision walking' thing to find Caroline?"

And when Catherine nods, Emma's frown deepens even further and her voice sounds astounded when she demands, "So why haven't you brought him in on this before – he could have saved us a hell of a lot of work and had Caroline home by now?!"

Looking like steam is about to come out of her ears, Catherine turns to stone and glares at Emma. "We already went to Farraday – it didn't work. I got nothing, nada, flaming zilch!"

"Ok, so now you've lost me," Emma slumps back in her seat and lolls her head to one side frowning up at Catherine. "If you already came up with nothing, why bother going back to the man?!"

"Because I'm doing it now – I'm connecting with Caroline," she explains. "I couldn't even do that when I went to see Farraday. I was almost totally blocked off to her. You see...you get it?"

Sitting up straighter in her chair, Emma gets her mobile out and could laugh at the look on Catherine's face. "Hi Sloane, Emma, we need Neil Farraday asap – could you possibly pick him up and bring him to our office?"

She listens while Sloane tells her that Lakelands isn't just around the corner from Sheriton and that she'll owe him big time for this. "Ok, so stay over at mine tonight and I'll make it up to you," Emma grins wickedly into the phone, then coughs to hide her embarrassment when she realises Catherine is listening. "Ok, so we'll see you soon, bye."

Not saying anything, Catherine just raises a brow and waits expectantly.

"He's going to pick Farraday up and bring him here," Emma tells her unnecessarily. And with a little blush she continues, "It'll be some time later this afternoon – so, if nothing comes of it, he'll probably finish his work at mine and stay over."

"Yes, I got that impression," Catherine smiles sardonically. "I'm going to phone Travis and let him know what we're going to try and make sure he's ok."

"The poor man must be going out of his head," Emma grimaces with sympathy. "I can't imagine what he's going through. And you, too," she adds, surprising Catherine.

Stopping on the way back to her desk, Catherine turns back to look at Emma and is glad to know that they are actually friends. She's had precious few of them in her life, till now.

"At first, I couldn't see past the panic – the physical pain I felt inside was almost debilitating," Catherine admits. "Now, I've managed to push that aside because my sister needs my brain to function in order to get her back home where she belongs."

Shaking her head in wonder, Catherine says, "It still hurts like hell – especially when I talk to our dad or Adrianne...but..." And Catherine shrugs, her unguarded expression telling Emma more than any words.

"You know, that's the first time you've ever opened up to me," Emma smiles encouragingly. "I'm glad to know that you can."

Blushing awkwardly, Catherine frowns deeply and continues to make her way to sit behind her desk. "I don't do 'confessions'..." she dismisses angrily, her usual response to feeling uncomfortable, "...so don't expect me to start indulging in 'girly chats'!"

When Emma laughs at her outraged expression, Catherine just ducks her head lower over her laptop.

Bloody hell! Are you suffering from verbal diarrhoea, or what, woman!

After giving herself time to settle down, Catherine does a round of phone calls to family. She repeats the fact, that they are working hard but there have been no major breaks as yet, to first Adrianne and then her dad. They are both so worried and Catherine feels guilty for not being able to give them any good news.

With Travis, Catherine gives him the same lowdown on the bare facts of their investigation, but adds, "I'm going to try again with Neil Farraday this afternoon – I think I might be able to get further this time – I'm getting through to Caroline a lot clearer and easier now."

It wasn't much to offer, she knows, but Travis' response had been positive and very encouraging.

He's trying desperately to be stoic through all this; if only I could give him something more solid to hang on to. It's only the girls who are keeping him sane!

With a groan of pain, Caroline tries to shift her weight for some relief. She can't move far, her limbs are so stiff and tied really tightly since Cherish Wade had added tape to her restraints.

"What are you doing?" Cherish snaps, coming back into the room. "Are you trying to escape, you wretched woman!"

Feeling weak and terribly tired, Caroline just closes her eyes and says, "No. Please, Cherish, I need water..."

But Cherish isn't listening; she has another voice whispering in her ears.

What does she think this is a bloody restaurant! We need to teach her a lesson – show her who's in charge, and who is going to be going back to a happy life with Travis!

"Yes, you're right...you're right," Cherish agrees with a spiteful chuckle. "But not now, I need to see Travis – we're getting on so well, he obviously still loves me."

Without a backward glance, Cherish leaves Caroline to suffer on her own. But having slipped into unconsciousness, Caroline isn't aware of how dire things are fast becoming.

The day is bright and Cherish is just so happy, her feet barely touch the ground as she walks the short distance to The Lovett Hotel.

Sliding both hands down her slender hips, Cherish straightens the pale blue pleated skirt of the dress she is wearing and tucks a wayward strand of hair behind her ears.

The hotel is busy and Cherish has to wait to speak to the receptionist. "Would you be kind enough to inform Travis Lovett that Cherish Wade is here for a visit?" she asks sweetly.

"Of course, madam," Jane smiles, and picks up the telephone to call up to the penthouse. "Mr Travis, you have a visitor in reception, sir – Ms Cherish Wade." Waiting for his reply, Jane keeps her eyes down to hide her confusion, but finally she hears him tell her to get Jake to escort Ms Wade to his private lift and put the code in for her.

Giving her a polite nod, Jake inputs the penthouse code without letting the lady see what he's doing. "There we go, madam..." he smiles when the lift doors open, "...Mr Travis will greet you in the penthouse."

Glowing with happiness, Cherish uses the mirror in the lift to check her appearance. "Oh, Travis...we're going to be so happy. I've always known you are special, and now we can spend the rest of our lives loving each other and..."

When the lift doors open and Cherish comes face to face with Travis in his familiar home, she smiles happily and immediately walks into his arms.

"I've missed you, darling," she croons, her arms encircling Travis's waist and her face pressed into his chest. "Are your parents around – I haven't seen them for a while?"

My parents – of course, they died after Cherish was hospitalised. But Cherish is sounding peculiar – like she only saw them a week or so ago.

"No, not just now," he tells Cherish, not sure what is going on and not wanting to upset her. "How are you, Cherish? You seem...happy," Travis smiles guardedly.

"Oh I am, Travis. You always make me so happy," she smiles up at him with her old sweetness.

The voice has gone quiet now, Cherish is so full of girlhood dreams that she isn't listening to anyone or taking notice of the changes in the penthouse.

When she had visited as Travis' girlfriend many years ago, the furnishings had been quality but very drab by comparison. But this doesn't seem to register with Cherish.

"I've always loved how big this room is – open plan living is so much fun," Cherish giggles girlishly, and moves to one of the large settees to sit down. Holding a hand out to Travis, she beckons him over.

"Travis, shall I get Sara's feed – she beginning to wake up and it's about...time," Ellisa hesitates when she spots the visitor on the settee.

"That would be fine, Ellisa," Travis nods, not making any move towards Cherish, who has let her hand fall to her side.

"And who is this?" Cherish demands, looking from the young woman and up at Travis.

"Cherish, would you like some tea – I'm sure Ellisa could arrange some for us?" he smiles, trying to divert her attention.

But Cherish is now glaring at Ellisa with open hostility in her eyes. Then she turns that glare on Travis and gets to her feet. "What on earth is going on – I've never known you to have a woman up here when your parents aren't home. Who is she, Travis?"

He can see what little control Cherish has, slipping as she becomes more and more confused and agitated.

"Cherish, this is Ellisa, my wife's personal assistant who is helping out with our girls while Caroline is away," Travis explains gently, deciding that to play along with her fantasy will only put them all in danger. *I need to pull you back to reality, try to make you see reason. But how?*

"Wife! Wife!" Her voice is getting higher and louder as the shock hits her, and when the twins wake and begin to cry in unison she appears to snap.

Pulling at her hair, Cherish screws her face up in an angry scowl. "No! No! This isn't right! I'm your fiancée, you said we were getting married..."

Ellisa looks to Travis for instructions, and he tilts his head towards the girls' bedroom indicating that she should go to them.

"Cherish, please, calm yourself and listen carefully to me," Travis croons gently, his deep voice soothing and calm.

She quiets, her hands still in her hair but no longer tugging at it frantically, and Cherish looks at him as if she has no idea how she came to be there.

"Travis...?"

"It's alright, Cherish. You've been unwell," he tells her, his slow smile just enough to offer reassurance. "I'll help you – we can visit the hospital to get your medication – you'll be absolutely fine in no time."

"Hospital!" she gasps, eyes wide and full of horror. And Cherish goes from quiet and still to panicked and aggressive in a millisecond.

Launching herself off the settee, Cherish pushes Travis to one side as though he weighs nothing at all, and punches the button to call the lift, then turns to glare at him. "You think you can lock me up again...you think you can have your fancy woman living with you again – but you're MINE!" she yells, then jumps into the lift and quickly presses the button for the ground floor.

Walking quickly through the lobby and into reception, Cherish bulldozes her way through people as if not seeing them.

When Jane tries to ascertain if she's alright, Cherish turns crazed eyes on her, frightening Jane into open mouthed silence.

Guests are protesting about the rude woman's behaviour, though none of them appear to have been hurt. And Jane's inaction is only momentary as her mind turns to her boss.

Oh my Lord...Mr Travis!

Picking up the telephone, Jane calls up to the penthouse and is relieved when Travis answers. "Ms Wade just left, sir – she appeared...distressed," Jane tells him warily. "Is everything alright, sir?"

"Yes, I'll deal with it. Did Ms Wade cause a disturbance on her way out?" he asks, recalling her fierce anger as she'd turned to glare at him before the lift doors had closed.

"A bit of one – some jostling of a group of guests," Jane admits with a grimace.

"Apologise and invite them to have dinner on the hotel," Travis instructs. "Thank you, Jane."

CHAPTER NINETEEN

"That was Travis..." Catherine tells the group of people gathered in her office, "...Wade just left in an extreme state of distress having visited him, out of the blue, and believing that they were still a couple." Looking to Linda, Catherine seeks her advice, "She seems to be slipping back to when she was a girl, pre hospitalisation – Travis doesn't think she has any hold on reality at all now."

"Then Caroline is in imminent danger," Linda confirms, deciding that being tactful just isn't an option at this time. "We have to get to her as soon as possible...or we could lose her..."

Catherine pales but doesn't lose focus. This is not the time to allow her emotions to dominate as they have in the recent past. "Neil, get over here and let's get started – we'll sit on the floor to make it easier, ok."

Sitting cross-legged opposite each other they reach out to join hands and begin the process of clearing their minds.

It has never happened this fast before – Catherine and Neil find themselves standing in an empty, cavernous room that had obviously been used in recent times for screen printing.

"That's what Caroline could smell," Catherine points to previously used containers of chemicals used in acid printing. "At least we know we're in the right place."

But there doesn't appear to be a smaller room leading off the one they are in.

"Caroline. Caroline," she shouts out loud, and the people gathered around them in the office jump at the unexpected sound of her voice. "Come on, Caroline...you need to guide my way...where are you?"

And then they hear a groan, but can't fathom where it is coming from. "Just make a noise if you can't speak – we can hear you somewhere nearby," she assures her sister. And sure enough, they hear another groan, this time more insistent, and follow it to the far corner of the room.

There is no door, the wall just appears to be continuous, but when you get near to the end you realise that it finishes short and there is a small room hidden behind it.

"Oh my Lord!"

Catherine has only seen and heard Caroline through her eyes and thoughts, until now she hasn't been able to see her in person and the sight is shocking.

Lying bound, hand and foot with tape over her eyes and mouth, on a concrete floor that is sapping her body's heat, Caroline is barely conscious.

There is nothing that Catherine can do to aid her sister at this point, she is there only in her mind and cannot interact with her surroundings.

"Caroline…I can see you sis' but I can't touch you, my hands just go right through you," Catherine tells her, having immediately tried to undo her sister's bindings. "I need to look around, find something that will tell us where this place is and then the police will come and get you, ok?"

No answer; not even a faint moan – Caroline has slipped deeper into unconsciousness.

"Neil, come on, we have to find something to identify where we are," Catherine demands, taking charge of the situation. "Are we ok to split up – I mean, I won't snap back, will I?"

"No, you don't need to be in close proximity to me while we are here," he explains. "It's our bond back in the office that is allowing me to help you do this."

Reassured, Catherine and Neil go off to search, frustrated that they can't pick things up to look beneath them for more information.

But then, Catherine finds a letter – it's scrunched up and stained with dye, but a name and address is just visible at the top of the open corner.

"Neil, get over here," she demands urgently. "Have you ever heard of 'Totally Cool Prints'? It appears to be the last company that used this place."

"Hey, I have," he smiles, and earns a scowl from Catherine. "I have a couple of t-shirts they produced – they're really cool," he mutters, tailing off at the look of disapproval she is giving him.

"Just look at this address, do you think this is where we are?" Catherine asks, impatient for his answer.

"Yes! That's right – it looked very different when they were selling out of here as well as printing the stuff to order on the premises," Neil recalls. "But that's the address alright!"

Frowning, Catherine looks around helplessly. "How the hell do we do this – I can't pick the letter up and I can't write anything down. Damn it, Neil, this is fucking useless!"

"Just calm down," he tries to tell her, but it isn't the right strategy to use with Catherine. "I mean, listen to me and do as I say," and her scathing stare seems to tone down, just a notch.

"I talk in my head – no voice for anyone to listen to back in the office," he clarifies. "But you still speak out loud – if you just read the address and ask someone back at the office to write it down they'll have the information they need to find Caroline."

"Ok, let's give it a go," Catherine nods, her piercing eyes focusing on the letter now instead of frying Neil where he stands.

But, just as she is about to read the address, Catherine and Neil listen and watch as someone barges into the building ranting and raving and pulling at their hair.

"Oh christ, she's completely lost it!" Catherine watches, wide eyed, as Cherish paces back and forth muttering profanities and rambling nonsensically.

But then, they cannot hear the other side of Cherish's conversation with the person egging her on.

At times of real stress, the voice in her head takes on a visual form that Cherish can see and react to, and she is thoroughly absorbed in some terrible argument.

I told you to get rid of her! I told you she'd be trouble! But no, you had to tie her up and keep her!

"I didn't want to lose Travis," Cherish shouts at the apparition that only she can see. "He...he...no...not wife...she isn't...can't be... She's deceived him; she's trying to steal him from me. But I won't let her!"

So what are you going to do? You can't leave her alive – she'll find a way to get back to him, to take Travis from us. You have to kill her, now while we have the chance.

"Us!" Cherish demands, turning on the apparition as if it has betrayed her. "Travis is mine!"

Yes, yes, he belongs to you – but not for much longer if the other one escapes!

"She can't escape, I tied her up tight," Cherish smiles manically. "No escape for the deceiver!"

"Deceiver...?" Catherine turns to Neil, but he just shrugs his shoulders.

Then suddenly Cherish is looking around the room and shouting to someone she can't see. "Who's there? I know you're there, come out where I can see you," she demands eerily.

"She knows we're here?" Catherine whispers to Neil, shocked by the thought.

"Mentally ill people are often more open to psychic phenomena," Neil explains. "It usually gets put down to

their illness when they try to tell anyone about it —
auditory and visual hallucinations are par for the course in
a lot of cases."

*You see, I told you, someone has come to set the
deceiver free! Kill her now, while you have the chance...or
you will lose Travis forever!*

The voice is cunning, using her fear of losing her
heart's love to convince Cherish that the dreadful deed
must be done, and it must be done now!

"No. No. I won't let you free her," Cherish looks wildly
around the room, searching for them, and actually walks
right through Catherine.

"Holy God!" Catherine gasps. Not that she actually felt
anything; it was just a queer and unreal sensation to see
someone do that.

Turning from them, Cherish moves to the hidden
room and starts bringing out the bottles of turpentine -
returning until all of the bottles are set out in the middle
of the room.

"Read the address, now!" Neil demands suddenly.
"And tell them it's urgent, I think Cherish is about to set
another fire with Caroline in the middle of it!" Watching
horrified, he sees Cherish struggling to drag Caroline's
body from the hidden room.

"No! We need to do something...we need to stop her," Catherine demands, terrified.

"We are not able to do anything," Neil explains more urgently. "We can't interact with our surrounding, Catherine. Just read the address and the Detective will send the local police to save your sister!"

Struggling to take her eyes off of what Cherish Wade is attempting to do; Catherine reads the address out loud and adds a description of what is currently going on.

Listening to Catherine, Emma gasps loudly and tears begin to fall in earnest. "Sloane, you have to do something...Caroline..." she pleads, desperate for this nightmare to stop before anyone else gets killed.

Moving to one side, Sloane takes out his mobile and calls it in, making sure that dispatch know the urgency of the situation.

"They're sending multiple units to the scene and alerting the fire department and ambulance services to attend, just in case," Sloane updates the rest of the group as he moves back to Emma's side.

Sitting on the floor behind Catherine, one leg on either side of her immobile form, Logan leans forward to put his arms around her, being careful not to break her contact with Farraday, just to hold her against his warmth and share their deep bond. "I'm right here, Catherine. I'm with you always," he tells her and knows, on some basic, primal level, that Catherine will feel his presence, his love and his strength and be able to draw on it if she needs to.

Moving quickly about the room, Cherish is piling up anything that she thinks will burn and, before long, has a small bonfire built.

Taking a bottle of the turps, she empties it over the stacked debris and throws the empty bottle onto the pile. Repeating this process, Cherish empties half of the turps onto the bonfire and stands back to admire her work.

More, it needs more, the voice urges Cherish on. *You want to make sure she burns, don't you?*

"Stop ordering me about!" Cherish shouts, making Catherine look around quickly for another person in the room. "I decide what we're going to do, not you, and I want the rest for the hotel – that's a fire I want to watch burn for a very long time," she sniggers, then laughs raucously.

"She's planning to set The Lovett on fire?" Catherine looks at Neil in astonishment. "But Travis...I thought she loved him?"

"I imagine she plans to keep him absent from the hotel in some way," Neil surmises. "I doubt he would be her target."

Sudden understanding dawns on Catherine and she determines to do something to stop Cherish.

If she managed to feel our presence once, maybe I can make her do so again.

And then she feels him – Logan is suddenly not only in her heart and mind but filling her with his strength and love.

Help me, Logan. I need to make her feel me – I need my presence to be strong and true...for Caroline!

Suddenly, Catherine can feel herself become 'more' and walks to where Cherish is still arguing with someone unseen and continuing to pile more rubbish on to the bonfire.

"Cherish Wade, stop what you are doing and listen to me!" Catherine demands, and is shocked when the demented woman does as she's told.

"I knew you were here..." Cherish turns about the room, not able to see who has spoken to her, "...you can't fool me. But you can't have her, she's mine and she's going to burn."

Having heard the police sirens signalling their arrival; Catherine pulls on everything she has to distract Wade and gain enough time for them to find Caroline.

Willing herself into existence, Catherine stands beside her sister and looks at Wade with furious blue eyes and says, "You will not touch me! My spirit forbids it," Catherine tells the terrified woman who has cowered back against the wall.

"If you are her spirit..." Wade points a shaking finger at Caroline then looks back at Catherine, whose features are identical in every way, "...then you must be already dead." Then Wade frowns, considering this information.

Take the turps and get out of here! We still have time to torch the hotel. She's dead, we don't need to bother with her anymore – but the deceiver's brats still live and they will take Travis away from you.

Looking warily at what she thinks is Caroline's spirit, Wade moves slowly towards the bottles of turps stood just behind where Caroline lays on the floor.

But Catherine, thinking that Wade intends to drag her sister into the bonfire and set light to it, steps forward and puts all her energy into her being.

Neil is stupefied by what he is seeing; Catherine is lit up like a Christmas tree, giving off an aura that causes Cherish to shrink back in fear.

The first police officer through the door also stops abruptly, his expression one of stunned disbelief. But in an instant he is in the room and making his way across to Cherish, talking to her in a gentle, reassuring voice. But every second or so, his eyes dart back to where he could have sworn a woman had been standing and had suddenly disappeared.

"Ms Wade...Cherish..." he calls to her softly, trying to gain her attention, "...I have a gentleman here who wishes to speak with you." Turning, he signals to Travis to step forward into view. "If you would just allow us to take Ms Lovett, you can have a private talk, if you wish?"

Mad eyes look from Caroline to Travis, and suddenly she just wants to be alone with her lover.

"Take her, but don't you come near me or else," and she grabs one of the full bottles of turps, undoes the top and holds up a cheap flick lighter, threatening to set the place alight.

Travis nods at the officer, having already planned to distract Cherish while the police rescue his wife. How he is going to get out is another matter – but at least Caroline would be safe, and that's all Travis cares about.

<u>CHAPTER TWENTY</u>

"No! Travis, no, you can't trust her," Catherine screams at him, but is unable to make him hear her.

Too exhausted from her previous efforts, Catherine can only watch as her brother-in-law puts himself in mortal peril.

Unsure of what to say now that she has Travis alone, Cherish watches him steadily as he approaches.

"You look tired, Cherish," Travis observes, not unkindly. "Won't you let me take you back to the hotel to look after you?"

His deep brown voice rumbles through her, taking Cherish back to when they were young and in love. "You want me to live with you there?"

Playing along with her assumption, Travis nods and smiles, "We can be happy, you and I, as we were always meant to be. Come, Cherish..." he beckons, holding a hand out to her, "...let us go home."

Smiling brightly, all madness gone from her beautiful face, Cherish begins to move forward, the bottle of turps and the lighter now held loosely at her side. "Yes, Travis, we should go home and tell your parents. Your mother will love organising the wedding. Maybe they will let us have it at the hotel?" she suggests, her brown eyes alight with the prospect of becoming his wife.

But just as she rounds the small bonfire in the middle of the room and reaches out to him, the voice in her head takes control and a high pitched screech rents the air.

"Cherish, NO!" Travis can do nothing but stand frozen to the spot as the love of his younger life jumps back and empties the bottle of turpentine all over her.

"You can't fool us..." Cherish's voice has changed, is full of anger and hatred, "...we know what you're trying to do! But we won't go back, and you can't make us," she screams.

Realising what she intends to do, Travis tries to dash around the pile of debris to get to Cherish.

A wall of flame is suddenly barring his way, and then a whoosh and an explosive force catapults him across the room.

"Mr Lovett?" A handful of police officers that had been holding back in the stairwell now flood into the room to see what is to be done. "Mr Lovett..." a young officer pats him down, swatting at small patches of flame on his clothing, "...we need to get you out of here!" And with that, a group of officers grab his arms and legs, hauling Travis from the room.

Catherine can barely believe what she is seeing — Cherish Wade is in flames, screeching wildly, still shouting obscenities at Travis and Caroline.

And then the terrible sight vanishes, Catherine's eyes no longer seeing the room, her body now slumped in Logan's arms.

As Neil Farraday comes back to himself, he looks grave and full of concern when he sees Catherine unconscious and Logan trying desperately to wake her.

"What did you do..." Logan demands, glaring hotly at Neil, "...why isn't she waking up?!"

Shaking his head sadly, Neil moves nearer to Catherine and places his hands either side of her head.

"What are you doing?" Logan snatches Catherine away from Neil's touch, afraid that even more harm will come to her.

"I need to try to get through to her — guide her back...if I can," he finishes quietly.

"IF you can?" Logan demands, outraged that Neil has put his wife in such peril. "You'd better make sure you put this right, Farraday, or I won't be accountable for my actions!"

Emma, Linda and Sloane are all watching on, horrified by Catherine's continued unconsciousness.

At Logan's words, Sloane takes a step nearer – he won't allow him to do Farraday harm – his ending up on a murder charge would hardly be justice after everything that's happened.

Allowing Farraday to replace his hands on either side of Catherine's head, Logan lets out a low growl of warning causing Farraday to look at him curiously.

Closing his eyes, Neil tries to join with Catherine again, searching her mind for a link. *Catherine,* he calls to her, but gets no response, *Catherine, listen to my voice! Focus on my voice and open your mind to me – it's time to go back. Let me help you, Catherine – Logan is waiting for you,"* he adds, hoping to trigger an emotional response that he can hone in on.

But Catherine's mind remains quiet and dark, leaving him no way in.

"I'm sorry..." Neil starts to say, as his hands fall away to his side – but he doesn't get to finish as Logan reaches to put his large hands about his neck.

"Noooo," Emma shrieks, her eyes wide with shock. "Logan, no!"

Linda moves forward and Emma immediately joins her, both of them hauling Catherine out of harm's way. The three men are rolling around on the floor like a pack of wild animals, Logan's roar as loud as any lion's.

His fists are ploughing into Neil Farraday; Sloane unable to drag him off.

Deciding that brute force isn't working, Sloane Shivers moves to the side demanding, "Do you want to end up behind bars for murder? Is that what Catherine would want?!"

The raucous sound of fighting has brought Henry up to the office, and he is astounded by what he sees.

"Son! What is this...what's going on?!" Henry demands, his eyes taking in Catherine's inanimate state and his son in the process of committing murder.

Logan hesitates; his hands now back round Farraday's throat and squeezing the life out of him.

"Your wife needs you, Logan — will you leave Catherine to die for a momentary satisfaction...?" Henry presses his point, having quickly assessed the situation.

The red rage begins to calm, clearing his mind and vision as a cold chill washes through Logan. Like a rag doll, he tosses Farraday aside in Sloane's direction, then hauls himself to his feet.

"Get him out of my sight before I finish the job!"

"Son?" Henry moves forward to put a hand on Logan's arm, their eyes meeting and holding for a moment before Logan moves to Catherine's side.

Linda has already got her fingers on Catherine's neck, feeling for a carotid pulse, when Logan joins her at his wife's side.

"Is she alive?" he asks, dreading the answer.

Nodding, Linda gives a small smile that offers only little reassurance. "Call an ambulance, her pulse is faint and thready – she could go into cardiac arrest at any time!"

With her mobile in hand, Emma signals that she is on the case and calls 999.

Taking Catherine in his arms, Logan rises with her limp body and carries her to their bedroom. Almost instantly he hears the boys wake and looks to Linda for help.

"Don't worry about the twins..." Linda touches Logan's arm to offer some comfort, "...your dad and I will take care of them."

When the paramedics arrive, Logan is forced to step away from Catherine – the very last thing he wants to do, and feels his heart pounding in his ears when they declare that she has arrested.

Activity around the bed suddenly doubles; sticky pads are applied to Catherine's chest and defibrillation paddles applied over them.

When the shock is applied, Catherine arches off the bed and Logan is frozen to the spot, staring uncomprehendingly at the nightmare scene.

"She's still in VF – we need to shock her again!" and the paramedic looks around the bed to make sure that no one is touching it before he sends another jolt of electricity through Catherine.

Again, her back arches off the bed and then slumps back when the paddles are removed.

A moment of silence endures, just a second, but it is filled with pain and panic for Logan.

"Ok, she's back in sinus rhythm," the paramedic declares, but the activity doesn't lessen. Lines are connected to Catherine's arm and fluids attached, then the paramedics strap her to a transport chair and move her quickly to the ambulance.

Climbing in beside her, Logan holds Catherine's hand, willing her to come back safely to him.

"We need you, Catherine. I need you," he declares fervently, raising her fingers to his lips.

Two days later and Catherine and Caroline are still unconscious. Both have been given CT scans and no brain damage has been detected in either of them.

The doctors are stymied, they've corrected Caroline's dehydration and begun enteral feeding, but nothing seems to be working.

Then Linda suggests moving the twins into the same room. "They have a very special bond..." she explains to one of the consultants, "...I think putting them in close proximity may help."

Raising a sceptical brow, the consultant considers the idea then instructs it to be carried out. "After all..." he smiles at Linda, "...we don't know everything about the body, let alone the mind. It's worth a try, at least."

Just minutes after the women are moved and their hands joined, they stun doctors and nurses alike when their bodies begin to synchronise.

"I've never seen anything like this..." the consultant says to his medical team, who are watching the vital signs monitors in disbelief, "...their vital signs are changing — heart rate, blood pressure and respiratory rate all appear to be adjusting themselves!"

"Yes..." the senior registrar agrees, "...and they are normalising – Ms Lovett's low blood pressure is rising and

Mrs Colson-Sayers' is coming down – I've never seen anything like this!"

"Jacobs..." the consultant turns to one of the house officers, "...start documenting this – I want starting figures times and end results – got that!"

"Already started," Jacobs blushes brightly, his reputation for being a 'details' man has earned him much teasing from the rest of the medical team. But this time he gets a nod of approval from the big boss himself.

"Good man, that's why you'll go far," the consultant tells the young man.

"I've brought the temperature probes up on the monitors now..." the nurse caring for the twins tells them, and points to the changing numbers, "...I attached them a couple of minutes ago – you see...their temperatures are equalising also!"

Caroline had been suffering hypothermia when she was admitted to the hospital – a warming blanket had been employed but she has been having some difficulty in maintaining her core body temperature.

Catherine's body temperature has been normal throughout; now it appears Caroline's is coming up to match it.

"Quite incredible! Jacobs, I want you to work with the nursing staff and document all cares given and vital signs for the next 48 hours," the consultant instructs. "I want every detail of any changes that occur, no matter how small, and the affects they have on both sisters, should any be seen. We'll review this again towards the end of that time."

"Yes sir!" Jacobs eagerly agrees. This is what he is good at and he's being given a chance to shine.

"I'll make sure you hand over to Channing – she's as hot on details as you are," the consultant frowns, considering his plan. Then, apparently satisfied, he leads the medical team on to review the next patient.

When Adrianne visits later that same day, she finds that her sisters have been moved into a side-room together and look like mirror images of each other.

The nurse looking after them greets Adrianne and places a chair at the side of Caroline's bed, the only side that a chair will fit into.

But Adrianne hesitates, wanting to hold both her sisters hands. "I'm sorry to be a bother but, do you think it would be possible to pull Caroline's bed a little further over this way," she indicates hopefully.

"Of course..." the nurse smiles and moves to carry out Adrianne's request, "...we kept them close together so that their hands could touch."

When the beds are separated, Adrianne moves her chair to sit between the beds and joins hands with both of her sisters. "I'm here, Catherine," and she gives her hand a comforting squeeze. Giving Caroline's hand a similar squeeze, she tells her, "I'm here for you too, Caroline. You both need to wake up now; your children are missing their mummies."

CHAPTER TWENTY-ONE

Doctor Jacobs duly notes down the changes that occurred in the vital signs of both patients immediately after they were parted. Then he does the same again when their sister takes her place and joins hands, forming a human chain.

Both their heart and respiratory rates had spiked during the separation, denoting a possible stress response, but had quickly normalised once the third sister had joined hands with them both.

It's like the circuit between the twins was broken and then completed again once the third sister linked her hands with theirs. It would be really interesting to see if the third sister's vital signs have aligned themselves with those of her sisters – but I suppose attaching a monitor to her would be too much to ask.

Still, she might be up for it!

"Err, Mrs Kingsley, isn't it? I'm Dr Jacobs," he introduces himself when Adrianne nods. "I'd like to explain something to you about your sisters' conditions," he tells her, and suddenly he notes a change in the monitors, the twins' heart rates are suddenly spiking.

Seeing Adrianne's look of alarm, he wonders if the monitors are actually picking up her reaction, rather than that of her sisters.

Excusing himself for a moment, Jacobs moves back to the table where he is documenting every detail and adds this event to the rest.

Once Jacobs has explained what he is doing, the importance of what he is documenting, Adrianne is reassured that nothing adverse is happening to her sisters. In fact, it sounds like they are gaining some celebrity among the hospital staff.

"What I was really hoping..." Jacobs begins again hesitantly, his cheeks heating and causing him great consternation, "...I mean, what I would like to ask..."

Adrianne smiles, immediately putting the shy man at his ease," Please, whatever you need, I'm sure my sisters would be pleased to cooperate."

"Well, it isn't actually them I'm thinking of," Jacobs tells her and receives a look of utter confusion. "I was hoping you would allow me to connect some basic monitoring equipment to you," and when Adrianne's smile slips and she sits back in her chair to look at him, Jacobs is certain that he has blown his big chance to impress the big boss.

"Why?" she asks, not at all sure what is going on. Not that she's worried about the actual monitoring – she's only just given birth to a baby and had been attached to the same type of monitoring then. But why – that is what's worrying her. *Do I look ill, or what?*

"This event is a clinical mystery – I'd like to see if the same kind of synchronicity is taking place in you," and he looks to their joined hands.

The penny drops with a clang, and Adrianne laughs at the thought of it.

"I doubt I have my sisters' abilities – they have a very special bond," Adrianne dismisses lightly.

"Would you be willing to put that to the test?" Jacobs challenges with a raised brow.

Actually, I'm not sure I want to. Feeling like the odd one out and knowing that I am are two very different things. How would I feel if I really am separate – would I feel alienated...isolated...?

Giving herself a mental shake, Adrianne gives the young doctor a determined smile. "Ok, let's do it!"

It doesn't take long to get the equipment set up and connected to Adrianne – then she, the nurse and Jacobs all watch the new monitor with growing anticipation – or dread in Adrianne's case.

Catherine's and Caroline's observations don't change at all, they are steady and stable at all times.

Allowing a couple of minutes for Adrianne to become accustomed to the equipment and settle down into a regular pattern, Jacobs begins documenting her vital signs along with those of her sisters.

Eventually Jacobs has to admit, the experiment has been a resounding failure. The twins are still synchronised, but Adrianne's vital signs are very different, expressing a good deal of stress.

"I'm sorry to have wasted your time..." he tells Adrianne, smiling apologetically, "...but it was worth a try. If you'll excuse me, I'll just document everything then I'll get rid of those leads."

I knew it – Catherine and Caroline are so close – I've never felt 'connected' as sisters the way they obviously are. But I know they love me...so why do I feel so sad?

For a while, Adrianne sits just holding her sisters' hands until her head starts to nod and she falls asleep.

The nurse decides to leave her for a while, knowing that the young woman has a newborn baby at home.

Having a 10 month old of her own, the nurse has a lot of sympathy for Adrianne.

Probably doesn't get much sleep, poor thing – and now all this worry on top of it, she's bound to be exhausted.

Stepping out of the room, the nurse goes to a nearby cupboard to fetch a fresh bag of fluid for Caroline.

On her return, the nurse observes the three monitors and is amazed by what she sees.

"Dr Jacobs...look," and she points to Adrianne's monitor, now showing exactly the same readings as her sisters.

Jumping up from his seat, Jacobs walks over to see for himself and he, too, is astounded by the evidence of his own eyes!

"Quick, you read out the numbers and I'll document them," he tells the nurse in a whisper so as not to disturb Adrianne, both of them now smiling with excitement. "Chapman will be ecstatic when he sees this!"

An hour later and Jacobs has something even more astounding to document. When Adrianne awakes so do Catherine and Caroline – all of them smiling as though they have a shared secret.

Just one weeks later all the sisters' children are gathered at Adrianne's house, their grandparents coming together to look after them for the afternoon.

It is the day of Cherish Wade's funeral, and Travis has spared no expense in making sure that she is laid to rest in a respectable and caring manner. He has taken sole charge of all the arrangements, wanting to do this last thing for a woman he once loved.

The few living relatives of the tragic young woman have come together at the church where Cherish is to be interred.

The sun is shining obscenely for such a solemn occasion, but it helps to lift the spirits of those in attendance.

Walking into the old church building, the chill is all the more noticeable in contrast to the mid-afternoon summer heat.

"This is pitiful," Adrianne observes as she and her sisters, along with their spouses walk up the aisle to the front of the church.

Only 5 other people have turned up for the funeral and it makes Cherish's passing feel all the more sad.

The minister taking the service greets them all with a sombre smile, and then he begins telling a tale of happier times when Cherish was a child growing up in Sheriton.

It is a revelation to the sisters – their impression of Cherish has been tainted by recent events, but now they are hearing what a happy caring child she had once been.

"Cherish had many dreams..." the vicar smiles, "...and they often changed, as most children's do. From wanting to be a nurse, to a teacher and even a fireman, I'm given to understand," and he chuckles at the thought.

"But as Cherish reached adulthood, she met and fell in love with a young man who she believed would be her entire future. They had been passing friends at school, but this was different, this was serious and they shared a love that it was hoped would take them on a new path together," and the vicar's smile falters as he recounts the rest of the story.

Caroline gives her husband's hand a reassuring squeeze and lays her head against Travis' shoulder.

"But it wasn't to be..." the vicar continues sadly, "...a terrible illness claimed Cherish; taking her from her family and the man she so loved. Schizophrenia is a long misunderstood illness that takes over a person's life to such an extent that they are no longer in control of their actions and need help and medication to aid them in coping with their changed life."

"Some sufferers are able to manage a regime of medication and counselling that returns them to a life with a good degree of normalcy. Others, like Cherish, are not so fortunate and need hospitalising for an extended period of time."

Taking the time to look at them all individually, the vicar wordlessly implores them to give Cherish their understanding.

"Are we not fortunate that we have our lives and our families to love and to enjoy – that we were not chosen by this terrible disease," he asks them quietly. "I'd like you to join me in thanking our Lord for his grace and mercy, his love and tolerance of our errant ways, and to ask him to take Cherish into his arms and give her peace, at last."

Beckoning them to stand, the vicar continues with the service, and then draws it to a close.

With the internment over, Travis talks with Cherish's family members and offers them to stay at his hotel overnight and use its facilities free of charge. But they want only to return home, and thank him for all he has done.

The journey back to Adrianne's home, is a quiet, contemplative one, each considering the vicar's words and the circumstances that had made Cherish who she was and influenced the way she acted.

Every one of them offers up thanks to whatever spiritual influence they believe in - even Robert, who doesn't have a religious bone in his body. And all are grateful to be able to return to their wonderful families.

CHAPTER TWENTY-TWO

It's the first time that all of the generations have been together in their entirety.

When the parents enter Adrianne's sitting room, they find the floor littered with their babies all having a nap.

"Oh, doesn't that look sweet," Adrianne croons softly, and turns to put a finger to her lips and shush the rest of her party into silence as they come in behind her.

"Jesus!" Catherine gasps and frowns, momentarily unsettled by the scene. "Looks like a maternity ward."

When Adrianne gazes up adoringly at Robert and says, "It makes you realise how wonderful it will be when we have three of our own," Catherine stares at her sister open mouthed.

"You did say you'd consider having another one," Logan reminds her, whispering close to Catherine's ear.

Swallowing hard, she looks up at her adoring husband and feels herself caving in. "Yes, I said I'd consider it – but do you really want a house full of those!" And she flicks a hand in the general direction of the sleeping babies.

"You don't fool me for an instant..." Logan grins, hugging Catherine to his side, "...I saw the dopey look on your face once you got over the shock when we walked in."

Giving him an elbow in his ribs, Catherine moves off towards her boys, sitting on the floor where they lay together on a blanket.

Sitting beside her, Logan sees a look of regret pass over Catherine's face. "You miss breast-feeding them, don't you?"

Without giving herself the time to cover her feelings, Catherine looks at Logan and nods. "That was our special time," she tells him sadly. "And I know baby formula is a really excellent substitute, but I wanted our boys to have the best – and Mother Nature seems to know what she's doing...most of the time."

Putting a hand to her stomach, Catherine grimaces and Logan watches her with growing concern. "You've not been feeling well all week – what's going on, Catherine?"

"I just got out of the hospital – maybe that has something to do with it," she suggests sarcastically.

"You were not well even before that episode – though no doubt it hasn't helped," Logan frowns, his concern growing despite Catherine's apparent dismissal of the subject.

Thankful for the interruption, Catherine picks Adam up as he begins to stir. "There's my boy," she smiles, laying him over her shoulder and nuzzling him with her cheek. "Always the first to wake – are you hungry, then?"

"There's a couple of bottle's made up in the fridge," Linda smiles over, watching the happy scene.

"You sit down with Adam, I'll get the milk," Logan offers, and strides off to the kitchen.

Getting herself comfortable in a large armchair, Catherine looks down into Adam's expectant eyes and can't restrain her smile.

So, your dad wants another one of you, does he? Well, I can't say I blame him – you are adorable - and your brother is just as cute.

Maybe another one wouldn't be so bad – I have to admit, Lakelands is just the place for a gaggle of children to grow up. And wouldn't that be fun – playing hide-and-seek at Lakelands would take on a whole new meaning.

Hmm, maybe we'll have to consider penning a play area off to start with?

When she sees Logan grinning down at her, Catherine frowns up at him. "What?!"

"You look beautiful," he tells her, and his grin stretches from ear to ear.

"Well you look crazy goofy," Catherine replies, though she can't help the smile that tugs at her lips. Then she recalls her thought about Lakelands. "We need a fenced-off area for the children to play in. If we're going to have another one we'll have children getting lost all over the damned place!"

Bending to take her face gently between his large hands, Logan places a tender kiss on her lips.

"I love you, woman! You're the best thing to ever happen in my life!" Only when Adam begins to object to not being fed, does Logan release Catherine's bewildered face and move reluctantly away.

I love you, too, Logan. And I promise to try harder, but feelings and emotions are difficult for me.

As she is feeding Adam, Catherine watches as her father discusses something with Henry, then gives a roar of laughter that is very quickly followed by all the women in the room shushing him.

He seems happy with Erin – maybe they'll make a go of it? I don't think mum would really mind – not after all the years dad stayed single, loving her all that time. He must have suffered a lot – I'm beginning to realise that now. I'd go crazy without Logan in my life.

Adrianne's adoptive parents don't seem to mind dad being in her life – though they were obviously nervous at the outset. They all seem to get along just fine; Lorna and Robert's mum have become firm friends, and his dad and ours regularly go fishing when they can.

Hell's teeth; this family lark is getting complicated – no wonder I struggle to keep up!

Adam has finished his bottle and Andrew is just waking up. Knowing his role in the feeding chain, Logan comes over to take Adam and gives Catherine another bottle of milk for Andrew.

She laughs, shaking her head in amazement, "It's like a flipping conveyor belt. Imagine what it will be like when we have three of the blighters?"

"Or four," Caroline speculates, her eyes wide having overheard the conversation. "You might get another set of twins – I'm surprised you're even willing to risk it!"

Frowning over at her twin, Catherine frowns and shakes her head, "The odds of that happening are 1 in 70,000 – I looked it up," she adds, smiling faintly over at Logan.

But Caroline is firmly shaking her head, "That only goes for identical twins – your next set might be fraternal, those odds are 1 in 12," she adds with a raised brow. "I looked it up, too – just in case!"

Travis looks at his wife with a worried frown, but then it changes into a bright smile.

"No! No way," Caroline wags a finger at her husband. "Just think about how much hard work it was for you while I was away – then double it!" she nods, both brows raised.

But Travis doesn't look perturbed at all, in fact, he's looking quite smug. "I thought I coped rather well, actually – with a little help, of course."

Turning to look at Catherine with accusing eyes, Caroline says, "There, now see what you've started!"

Adrianne is chuckling to herself, watching her sisters battle it out. *Back to normal, then. I've missed their tussles – I was frightened of losing them both for a while, and I couldn't bare that!*

Since the hospital testing, Adrianne has felt closer to her sisters, having previously felt somewhat separate from them.

Oh, she'd always known they were linked, as all sisters are, but she had wanted more than that – she had wanted to be a part of their special bond, and now she knew that she was.

If it hadn't been for them both being in the hospital at the same time and linked up to those monitors, I may never have found out. Dr Jacobs was very astute and deservedly received a lot of praise for his intuitive thinking from his boss.

Of course, Catherine and Caroline both balked at the idea of becoming part of an ongoing research project – but I think it might have been interesting.

"What are you looking so pensive about?" Catherine frowns over at Adrianne.

"Nothing. Well...just the hospital...you know...Dr Jacobs," Adrianne recalls haltingly.

Her frown deepens as Catherine recalls the good doctor and his eager consultant friend. "Why, you know we're not going there – right?"

Shrugging, Adrianne just blinks back at her sister then says, "You can't say it wasn't cool, what happened. It might be interesting to find out what else we can do when we all three put our minds to it?"

But Catherine sits further back in her seat, looking at her baby sister like she's grown a second head. "Not a chance! You really want someone attaching leads to you, monitoring you like a lab rat?"

"I hadn't really thought of it like that..." Adrianne draws her brows together considering the idea, "...but I doubt it would be all that bad."

Looking at Caroline and shaking her head in dismay, Catherine says, "Are you listening to this? If she wasn't already married I'd think our little sister had a thing for that Dr Jacobs!"

Choking on his tea, Robert quickly gets to his feet looking disapprovingly at Catherine then frowning deeply at Adrianne.

"Down boy!" Catherine chuckles at Robert's look of out-and-out consternation. "I said 'if she wasn't already married'," Catherine reiterates patiently. "You already know she's completely gone over you!"

Moving his head close to Catherine's ear, Logan whispers into it. "That wasn't very nice – you should know better than to tease a man like that – he's just as crazy about Adrianne as she is about Robert!" But he is smiling when Catherine turns to look at him.

"He's a big boy, he can take a joke!" But Catherine watches as Adrianne takes Robert's hand and gives it a reassuring squeeze.

Hell, it was a joke, what's he getting all bent out of shape for? I'll never get the hang of this family stuff...someone will always take offence at what comes out of my mouth, even if I don't mean anything by it!

"Stop worrying..." Logan smiles, taking her hand and holding on to it, "...you're doing just fine."

"What; are you a mind reader now?" she asks, dumbfounded by his perception.

"I know you better than you know yourself, that's all." Logan gives the hand he's holding a light squeeze and raises it to his lips for a kiss.

"I don't want to mess this up," Catherine admits, gesturing with her chin to all the family members gathered in the sitting room. "I know I'm not great with this stuff, but I really don't want to lose any of them."

"Just be yourself," Logan advises. "I love who you are and they will, too, if you let them."

<u>EPILOGUE</u>

The day has been a difficult one for Catherine; not used to dealing with her emotions she has had them churned up every which way in a short span of time.

The morning had been lovely, spending time at Adrianne's house with family before they had had to leave for Cherish Wade's funeral. And then the sadness of the funeral service; trying to sort out how she felt about Cherish in the light of all she now knew.

The evening had been better, though she'd still managed to get confused about how to deal with family members, how to be herself without causing offence when none was meant.

I suppose I'll get the idea one day. But I don't want to bring Adam and Andrew up to be as awkward with people as I am. They're so innocent...so open to the influences around them...to my influence...

"Will you stop frowning at them..." Logan puts an arm across Catherine's shoulders and hugs her to his side, "...if the boys wake up they'll think their mummy is cross with them."

"You see!" Catherine lifts terrified eyes up to Logan and then turns into him, wanting to climb inside where she can feel safe and loved. "And you want us to have another one – I'll never get this right – it just doesn't come naturally to me!"

But Logan won't hear of Catherine speaking badly of herself, and gives her shoulders a gentle shake. "Stop this, you are a wonderful mother! Our boys know you love them, care for them and want them in your life – isn't that all that counts, all they need to grow up feeling safe and happy?"

Pulling her into his arms and resting his cheek on top of her head, Logan's heart breaks for the child Catherine had once been. "Isn't that all you would have wanted?" he asks gently.

Then it's as if a bright light goes on in her head – yes, that was all she'd ever wanted, and she could give that to her sons with more besides. After all, she's got Logan to help her along the way, and if he doesn't know about happy childhoods no one does!

"Oh hell!" Tearing out of Logan's arms, Catherine bolts for the bathroom, a hand over her mouth, and vomits profusely into the toilet.

"Damn it, Catherine, you can't go on like this. I'm going to call the doctor," but Logan doesn't move until Catherine is feeling better.

"It's just a stomach bug — it's going around," she dismisses, getting to her feet and leaning over the sink to rinse her mouth out.

"Well, I'm not so sure," Logan frowns, worried by her pallor. "It wouldn't hurt for the doctor to take a look at you." And before she can protest further, Logan strides out of the bathroom and makes his way downstairs.

Catherine teeters over to their bed, falling back on it feeling washed out and a little dizzy.

Might not be a bad idea after all — I can't remember ever feeling this ill!

But when the doctor arrives, it doesn't take long for him to diagnose the problem. "Ah yes, just as I suspected..." he grins at the strip having dipped it into the urine sample Catherine has provided, "...you're pregnant, m'dear." And the doctor smiles like he's just announced that Christmas has come early.

"WHAT?!"

*****

If you have enjoyed this book, please leave a review at the place of purchase. Thank you.